Redeeming the Rancher
Deb Kastner

HARLEQUIN® LOVE INSPIRED®

Recycling programs
for this product may
not exist in your area.

 TM LOVE INSPIRED BOOKS

ISBN-13: 978-0-373-87897-0

REDEEMING THE RANCHER

Copyright © 2014 by Debra Kastner

www.Harlequin.com

Printed in U.S.A.

"I'm amazed at how you've turned these kids around."

Griff shook his head and grunted softly. "I remember how unruly they were at that first dinner with you."

Alexis choked on a laugh. "Them? I remember how unruly *you* were at that first dinner."

Griff blushed. "Touché."

"You've improved some upon acquaintance." Her lips quirked.

He smiled crookedly, his gaze warm and inviting. "You haven't."

"Gee, thanks," she quipped back at him. The way he was looking at her was causing her stomach to do all kinds of crazy somersaults.

"And by that," he drawled lightly, "I mean you are already perfect the way you are."

"Flattery, my dear man, will get you everywhere."

"Is that so?" He planted his cowboy hat on his head and winked. "I'll have to keep that in mind."

"Don't get lost," she teased.

"Same to you. I know how massive piles of paperwork can bury a person."

"I won't," she murmured belatedly as she watched Griff walk away.

Even as she said it, she knew it wasn't quite true. She *was* getting lost, but it wasn't the paperwork she was worried about.

She was in danger of losing her heart.

Books by Deb Kastner

Love Inspired

A Holiday Prayer
Daddy's Home
Black Hills Bride
The Forgiving Heart
A Daddy at Heart
A Perfect Match
The Christmas Groom
Hart's Harbor
Undercover Blessings
The Heart of a Man
A Wedding in Wyoming
His Texas Bride

The Marine's Baby
A Colorado Match
Phoebe's Groom
The Doctor's Secret Son
The Nanny's Twin Blessings
Meeting Mr. Right
†*The Soldier's Sweetheart*
†*Her Valentine Sheriff*
†*Redeeming the Rancher*

*Email Order Brides
†Serendipity Sweethearts

DEB KASTNER

lives and writes in colorful Colorado with the Front Range of the Rocky Mountains for inspiration. She loves writing for Love Inspired Books, where she can write about her two favorite things—faith and love. Her characters range from upbeat and humorous to (her favorite) dark and broody heroes. Her plots fall anywhere in between, from a playful romp to the deeply emotional. Deb's books have been twice nominated for the RT Reviewers' Choice Award for Best Book of the Year for Love Inspired. Deb and her husband share their home with their two youngest daughters. Deb is thrilled about the newest member of the family—her first granddaughter, Isabella. What fun to be a granny! Deb loves to hear from her readers. You can contact her by email at debwrtr@aol.com, or on her MySpace or Facebook pages.

Blessed are the poor in spirit,
for theirs is the kingdom of heaven.
Blessed are those who mourn,
for they shall be comforted.
Blessed are the meek, for they shall inherit the earth.
Blessed are those who hunger and thirst for
righteousness, for they shall be filled.
Blessed are the merciful, for they shall obtain mercy.
Blessed are the pure in heart, for they shall see God.
—*Matthew* 5:3–8

To Natasha Kern, my fabulous agent.
I'm so grateful for all the invaluable career guidance
you offer. You are a special and remarkable person
who is such a blessing to me in so many ways.
Thanks for believing in me.

Chapter One

Alexis Granger awoke to the smell of bacon and the tinny sound of pots and pans being shifted around in one of the kitchen cupboards. It might have been a pleasant surprise—if it wasn't for the fact that she lived alone.

With a start, she bolted out of bed, shakily wrapping a plush magenta-colored cotton robe around herself. She reached for her cell phone, which she usually kept on the nightstand, but it wasn't there. Her pulse ratcheted up right along with her thoughts. Where was her stupid phone? In her purse? Her coat pocket? Not good either way, since she routinely dumped them both in an inglorious heap on one of her kitchen chairs.

Her heart slammed in her chest as she looked around for anything she could use as a weapon against the intruder. In a panic, she swiped the largest item from her vanity and tucked it into the pocket of her bathrobe.

Oh, why didn't she keep a baseball bat by her bed?

Maybe because she didn't play baseball. And maybe because she resided in small town Serendipity, Texas. Crime was virtually nonexistent here. Only businesses secured their doors at night. Regular townsfolk rarely bothered to lock their cars, much less their houses. There was simply no need.

At least until now there wasn't. She sucked in a breath and held it. She *had* locked her door last night, hadn't she?

Yes. Of course she had. Or at least, she thought she had, since her ranch was also technically a non-profit ministry. Out of habit, if nothing else. *Oh, Lord, please let there be a rational answer.* But how else would someone have gotten in? Only her twin sister, Vivian, had a key.

Vivian.

Alexis let out the breath she'd been holding and her shoulders sagged in relief.

Of course. It had to be Vivian, even though Alexis hadn't expected to see her. Vivian was busy in Houston trying to get her new business off the ground and didn't have time to make the commute home more than a few times a year, but it was the only explanation that made sense.

For about one second.

Until she remembered that Vivian could not and did not cook.

At all. Ever. Period. Exclamation point.

Alexis dearly loved her sister, but she had no qualms admitting that the woman couldn't even boil water, much less cook bacon.

Then again, house thieves didn't pause to cook themselves a meal, either; at least none that Alexis had ever heard of.

Rational explanation, Alexis, she coached herself. *Don't panic. Don't freak out.*

Despite her efforts to be quiet, she couldn't contain the shaky laugh that tittered from under her breath, more nervous than amused, as she pictured a thief cooking breakfast in her kitchen. Barefoot and silent against the hardwood floor, she crept down the hallway toward the kitchen. The light was on, bacon was crackling on the stove and *someone* was humming.

A *male* someone.

Definitely not Vivian, then.

Alexis plastered herself to the wall, her breath coming in short gasps, her skin burning as if it was on fire. Even though she'd doubted the mystery intruder was Vivian, she'd still held out hope that there was nothing more sinister at work here than her sister fresh off a cooking class. But there was a man in her kitchen. And he appeared to be making himself at home.

What on earth?

Her pulse was pounding in her ears, nearly drowning out the sound of the mystery man. She was going to be in full-out panic mode if she hesitated much longer. Before she could think better of it, her fist circled around the makeshift weapon in her pocket and she sprang forward, brandishing the flat-iron wand in front of her like a sword.

"Who are you and what are you doing in my house?" she demanded with a good deal more bravado than she actually felt. If her voice came out a little high and squeaky, who could blame her?

The tall man hovering over the oven had been humming a pleasant tune to himself, but when he heard her voice he jumped back in surprise. He dropped the tongs he was holding and they clattered into the pan, spraying grease over his exposed left hand. He howled in protest and shook his wrist, then nursed his knuckle between his lips.

"Who am I?" he growled as he swiveled around to face her. "The better question would be…" The man's sentence drifted off into a strained silence and his dark brows lowered over gray-blue eyes. He shook his head, clearly bewildered.

"I asked you a question." Alexis lifted her weapon and took a defensive stance.

"Vivian? What are you doing here?" He hesitated a moment, his head tilting as he scrutinized her features. Uncertainty flashed in his eyes. "You're not Vivian."

Alexis sighed in relief and let her posture relax a bit. If the man knew her sister, then he probably wasn't a thief, although what he was doing making breakfast in *her kitchen* was still a mystery.

That said, she was impressed that he could tell her apart from Vivian. Most folks couldn't, at least not right away. It wasn't the first time she'd ever been mistaken for her twin sister and it probably wouldn't be the last. But she reminded herself not to give him too much credit. Since this man knew Vivian, he'd probably realized his mistake in calling Alexis by her sister's name as soon as he saw the complete lack of recognition on her face.

He was clearly out of his element, and not just because he was cooking up a meal in her kitchen as if he owned it. She guessed him to be in his mid-thirties and well-to-do. Thick dark hair threaded with the occasional touch of silver lent him a sophisticated air. Everything about the guy screamed *city boy,* from the spit-shine of his black cowboy boots to the designer scarf draped around his neck.

Designer clothing. On a guy. In Serendipity, Texas. He might as well have a Kick Me sign on his back. Men around here wore the scuffs in their boots like trophies.

"Alexis," she corrected. "Grainger. Vivian's twin sister."

"Alexis? *A-Alex*?" he stammered. "I… I'm, uh…"

"Confused, obviously." No one ever called her *Alex,* for one thing.

He nodded adamantly. "Yes, there is that. Were you—" he gestured toward her hand, one corner of his lip rising "—planning to stab me with your curling iron?"

Heat flooded her face as she hastily lowered her "weapon." She stuffed the flat-iron wand back into her bathrobe pocket, frantically looping the uncooperative tail around her palm. The cord stubbornly refused to follow and it took a humiliating length of time to complete the action. Her cheeks were positively burning by the time she finished.

"Yes. No," she stammered, shaking her head and scowling at the unwanted intruder. So he wasn't a random stranger but rather a friend of her sister's. That didn't mean he was welcome to barge into her home at a ridiculous hour of the morning. "Maybe. I thought you were a burglar."

Alexis didn't like the way the stranger flustered her with his sharp gaze. She liked it even less when he burst into laughter at her expense.

"Lady, if I was intent on swiping your possessions or causing you bodily harm, you would have been a lot smarter to sneak out the front door, get yourself to safety and call the cops on me. I'm guessing most criminal types wouldn't be deterred by your curling iron, no matter how bravely brandished."

His eyes flooded with amusement, but there was something else there, too.

Admiration.

The nerve of the man.

"Well, you're not here to steal my things or to hurt me, now, are you?" she demanded, annoyed that she continued to wrestle with the ridiculous inclination to defend her actions. Why should she? *He* was the one who was trespassing.

"No, ma'am, I'm not."

"It's a good thing for you I didn't call the police or you'd be in handcuffs right now. You should be thanking me, not giving me a hard time."

"Thank you," he said, sounding as if it were more of a concession to her than a heartfelt expression of gratitude. His lips quirked as he wiped his greasy palm against the black denim on his thigh. He extended his hand. "Griff Haddon, at your service."

"At my service? Really? I was under the impression you were helping yourself to breakfast." She ignored his outstretched hand and crossed her arms, not caring if the gesture looked defensive. Why should she care what he thought?

"I brought my own food." He gestured to a canvas bag tipped flat on the counter, spilling a carton of eggs and a loaf of bread.

"How reassuring."

He frowned. "Obviously there's been a misunderstanding here."

"Oh, I believe I *understand* just fine, or at least I can take a good stab at it. If I don't miss my guess, you're making yourself at home in my house because of something my ditzy sister said or did. What's lacking here is *communication,* a fact I'm going to rectify at my earliest convenience. I have a few words to exchange with my dear sister. I'm assuming she loaned you the key to our house?"

He scoffed and shook his head. "I'm glad you seem to think you've got a handle on what's happening, because I certainly don't. Yes, your sister gave me the key to the house, but in my defense, I was given to understand it would be empty. And for the record, I thought Vivian's sibling was a guy."

"I'm not, obviously."

"Obviously," he agreed wryly, his gaze altering as he swept a glance over her that made her skin prickle. She was relieved when he shifted his attention back to the stove and the bacon, which had burned down to shriveled, blackened crisps. Smoke was billowing from the pan. Griff snapped the knob on the burner off with a grunt.

"I'm surprised the fire alarm didn't go off," she said with a chuckle. Not that she'd noticed the food smoking any more than he had. She'd been too intent on Griff's presence to pay attention to anything else. Her house could have blazed down around them and she would have been oblivious.

"Sure, just rub it in," he muttered crossly as he wrapped a towel around the handle and removed the skillet from the burner. "There goes my breakfast, and after I drove half the night to get here in the first place," he added in disgust. "Oh, well. It is what it is. Where do you keep the trash can?"

Alexis leaned her hip against the table. Now it was

her turn to be amused. "Under the sink. But there's no sense throwing perfectly good meat away, even if it's burned to a crisp." She couldn't help but rub it in a little bit. "I've got a few dogs out back that'll be happy to chow down on that bacon. If you hand me the skillet I'll take care of it."

"Dogs, huh?" he said, gingerly transferring the pan to her, towel and all. "Good thing I didn't run into them. They probably would have believed I was an intruder, as well."

"Good thing," she agreed, opening the back door and depositing the contents of the skillet into one of the dog dishes just to the right of the door. Good thing for him, anyway. In her mind, he *was* an intruder of sorts, even if he had no intention of making off with her flat-screen television. He was lucky she wasn't the type of woman to sic her dogs on him.

"Coffee cups?" Griff asked when she returned. "Once I've got some caffeine in me, I'll explain what I know and maybe you can fill in the rest. After that, I guess we'll decide what we're going to do about this… situation."

She pointed to the cabinet above the microwave. What did he mean, decide what they were going to do? He was going to leave, thank you very much, and the sooner, the better—like, as soon as he had coffee in his system.

"It's hazelnut coffee. Cream or sugar?"

"Black, thank you."

He retrieved two mugs and poured the steaming coffee, then offered her one and gestured her to a seat on the bench side of the small breakfast nook table she kept in one corner. The larger table, where she usually took meals with her kids from the ranch, was located in the dining room. Her house was usually brimming with troubled teenagers, but this was the weekend between Mission Months and all was uncharacteristically quiet.

He waited until Alexis was seated before sliding into the chair opposite her and capturing her gaze with his.

"So let me get this straight," Alexis began, diving straight to the point. "Vivian loaned you her key and led you to believe the house was vacant." She cupped her mug in both hands and breathed in the rich hazelnut scent. "And you're looking for—what? A vacation? Some time away from the hustle and bustle of Houston?"

The left side of his lips twitched. "It's a little more complicated than that." He threaded his fingers through the tips of his dark salt-and-pepper hair, spiking the ends even more than they already were. "I'm looking to settle down, take a permanent vacation from the rat race, so to speak. Buy a ranch. Raise some horses."

He was a little too young to be thinking of retiring. In fact, he was a *lot* too young. Yet the sheer determination on his face gave Alexis no room for doubt that he meant what he said. If he was looking for peace and quiet, Serendipity was the perfect town for it—but really, what could this city boy possibly know about ranching? He would crash and burn in a week on a working ranch.

Wait. He wanted to buy a *ranch?*

Her heart sank. Oh, no. What had Vivian done?

"You're not thinking of buying Redemption Ranch, are you?" Alexis's voice squeaked out an octave higher than usual. With the financial troubles she'd been facing recently, losing her childhood home was at the fore-

front of her mind. Unless she could find a new source
of capital, there was a very great possibility her worst
case scenario was about to become a reality and she
wouldn't be able to afford to keep the place running.
But she wasn't ready to sell yet—or *ever,* if she could
avoid it. Ugly knots formed in her gut. Surely her sister
hadn't suggested that their land might be for sale. Yes,
the land belonged to both of them but Alexis was the
one who was actually doing something with it. Vivian was self-absorbed, but not so much that she didn't
understand what the ranch meant to Alexis.

No ranch, no ministry.

Alexis had done everything in her power to see that
Vivian could follow her dreams. She'd sacrificed everything—possibly even her own hopes and plans. It
looked that way right now, in any case.

Griff chuckled and held up a hand, bringing Alexis's
attention back to the present. "As I assured you earlier, I'm not here to swipe anything, and I'm not the
least bit interested in your home, stealing *or* buying.
Vivian told me all about the area, and it sounded like
the perfect place to settle down. I'm looking for something in or around Serendipity. Vivian kindly offered
to allow me to stay at the ranch while I searched for a
place of my own."

"I see," Alexis murmured, chewing on her bottom
lip as her thoughts flew in several directions. While it
was typical of her flighty sister to offer help without
really thinking through the consequences, it seemed a
little extreme for Viv to lead Griff to believe the house
was vacant. She knew perfectly well that Alexis lived
on the premises—not to mention that the ranch was
generally overrun with teenagers. And then there was

the odd addition of Vivian referring to her as *Alex*. That just wasn't right. She had never called her *Alex* before in her life.

What possible reason could Vivian have for such a deception? Something wasn't adding up. Unfortunately, Alexis never had been all that proficient with math, even the emotional kind. She was flummoxed.

What a mess.

The worst of it was the preposterous tug of guilt *she* was feeling for the way Viv had put the poor man out. Alexis almost felt as if she owed Griff something to make up for her sister's lack of foresight. It wouldn't be the first time she'd had to clean up her ditzy twin's messes.

She glanced at the clock on the stove. She had a phone call to make—from an irate sister to an imprudent one. She wanted answers, and she wanted them now.

But first she had to decide what she was going to do with Griff. He was definitely the most immediate problem. Vivian had given him some impossible promises, and it wasn't Griff's fault he'd been duped into believing her when she'd said he could stay at the supposedly vacant ranch house.

Then again, it wasn't exactly Alexis's responsibility, either. Why should she suffer for her sister's lack of common sense and be forced to try to find a place for this city slicker to stay?

And yet here she and Griff were, both in a pickle, and Vivian was, as usual, nowhere in sight.

One thing was certain. Griff couldn't stay at the Grainger house.

"What's the frown for?" he asked, intently studying her face.

"Just trying to figure out how to keep everybody happy here."

He chuckled. "Good luck with that. Talk about a sticky situation."

"No kidding." Alexis ran a hand down her face. How was she supposed to tell him he'd come all this way for nothing?

"You're trying to figure out how to send me packing," he guessed, though he made the statement with a smile.

She hesitated. "Well—yes. Politely," she admitted. "I'm sorry, but Vivian's put me in an impossible situation here. Not to mention what she's done to you. The way I see it, you have two options—go back to Houston or find somewhere else to stay in the area. And, quite frankly, there aren't a lot of choices here in Serendipity."

"Cut to the chase, why don't you?"

Alexis cringed. "Sorry. I know I'm blunt. I've never been the type to beat around the bush when I have something to say."

"You call it like it is. Nothing wrong with that."

Unless you're trashing a man's plans.

Alexis gulped at her coffee and struggled to regain her equilibrium.

"Hotel?" he suggested, tipping his chair back onto two legs and threading his fingers behind his neck.

"Sorry, no such thing in Serendipity. We don't have enough visitors in town to warrant such an extravagance. You won't find one within an hour's drive. However, the Howells have a nice bed-and-breakfast located across town. It's still a little early in the day, but I'm guessing they're up for church by now. Would you like me to give them a call?"

Griff nodded in agreement and rose to refill their coffee mugs while she stepped out of the room to phone the Howells. She was back less than a minute later with bad news.

"Well, we can scratch that idea. The Howells are booked solid for the next month. It's family reunion season, and if there's one thing Serendipity folk celebrate, it's family."

Griff set her refilled cup in front of her, slid back into his seat and stretched his arm across the back of the chair next to him. "I know this sounds unconventional, but do you have a spare bedroom I could use? I promise I won't be in the way, and I'll be out of your hair as soon as I can secure a place of my own. I'll even cook you breakfast if you'd like." The confident grin he flashed her exposed even teeth and a dimple on his right cheek. He looked like a man who never heard the word *no*.

He was in for a disappointment.

"Absolutely out of the question." She didn't even need a moment to think about it. The man had no idea what he was asking. Zero. Zip. None.

He raised his eyebrows, a glint in his eyes. She couldn't decide whether he was shocked by her outburst or was silently urging her to continue. Maybe a little of both.

She pressed her lips together and shifted her gaze over his left shoulder. Out the kitchen window gray doves were clustering near a feeder on her deck. A sign of peace amid a moment of tension. God's silent reminder. Alexis took a deep breath and prayed for guidance.

There were dozens of reasons why Griff couldn't stay at the house. She ticked them off in her head.

He wasn't family, for starters. Serendipity was a painfully small town where the gossip mill was concerned. Alexis didn't want to risk even the appearance of impropriety. And despite his reassurance that he'd stay out of her way, she knew herself well enough to know she would feel obligated to treat him like a guest. Adding one more mouth to the supper table wouldn't be much of a hassle, but squiring him around town while he got his bearings and keeping him entertained here at the ranch was another thing entirely. No matter what Griff said to the contrary, he would be a problem for her.

Last—or maybe it should have been listed first— she had another group of teenagers arriving for boot camp on Monday. She ran Redemption Ranch as an alternative to community service for troubled teens facing misdemeanors, a chance to change their lives for the better. Her hands were full. And so was her life.

She felt sorry for the man, but then, it really wasn't her fault he was in this predicament, nor was it her problem to fix.

At least in theory.

In practice, she had a man curiously staring at her over the breakfast table, apparently waiting for her to pull a bunny out of a hat…or something. Unfortunately she was fresh out of rabbits. She clasped her cup in both hands and squarely met his gaze.

"I've got to be honest with you, Griff. I don't have any idea what I'm going to do with you."

* * *

Griff locked gazes with the woman sitting across from him, her hands clenched so tightly around her coffee mug that her fingers were quivering. He was afraid the glass might shatter under the pressure she was exerting on it.

She didn't know what to do with him? *He* didn't know what to do with *her.* The last thing he'd expected to find when he'd come to Serendipity was a woman living in the "vacant" house he was supposed to be borrowing. He didn't know who'd been more shocked by their first meeting—Alexis thinking he was an intruder in her home, or him being surprised by a wild woman brandishing a curling iron. His knuckles still smarted from the splattered grease. But once the surprise had faded, disgruntlement had sunk in. The situation was hardly his fault. He'd acted in good faith, believing he had a confirmed place to stay. He couldn't be blamed for Vivian's deception. And in spite of it all, he was trying to be reasonable, trying to compromise.

One thing was for certain—Alexis Grainger hadn't left much bargaining room.

"No room for negotiating?" he suggested mildly. He'd been successful in his career as venture capitalist for a reason. He'd learned to keep his emotions in check, to always be confident and that it never hurt to ask.

"Absolutely none whatsoever."

Then again, asking for what he wanted could be a pointless gesture.

"Well, I'm not going back to Houston without finding what I came here for." He wasn't going back to Houston at *all*. He set his jaw. She wasn't the only one who could be stubborn. "It appears to me that your sister pulled a fast one on both of us."

"Says you." Alexis sniffed and shrugged offhandedly. "From my perspective, you're the one who got duped."

Griff's dander rose. *Duped?* Was that how she saw him? As a man easily swayed by a pretty face? Did he have it written on his forehead, or was it just part of a woman's natural mystique to be able to read a man like an open book?

It wasn't that long ago that he'd made the mistake of taking the word of a manipulative woman at face value. He'd believed himself to be less trusting now. Wiser. And yet apparently he hadn't learned his lesson at all. Though he still had no idea what her motive for all of this was, he couldn't deny that he'd stepped right into Vivian's scheming trap with eyes wide open. Now her beautiful twin considered him a chump.

If the shoe fit...

He'd already gone down that road and was the not-so-proud owner of the T-shirt. Color him a slow learner.

"No, I don't think so." He wasn't answering her so much as reprimanding himself, and didn't immediately realize he'd spoken aloud—not until Alexis lifted a high-arching blond brow in response.

"No? What do you mean, *no?*"

"Look, I don't mean to be difficult, but I really need to stay in Serendipity, to do this one thing for myself. I can't even begin to describe how important this is for me." It wasn't as if he could head back to Houston with his tail between his legs. He couldn't, and he wouldn't. It wasn't even an option for him. He'd put his apartment on the market and had his things placed in storage until he could move them out to whatever property he purchased. Decisive action had always been his trademark. Once he'd made the decision to leave Houston behind, he'd shut down his life there in record time.

He hadn't ever wanted to be a part of the wealthy, high-society scene to begin with, and now? Well, never again. His ex-girlfriend Caro had singlehandedly shredded everything he'd worked for his entire life, everything that mattered to him both personally and professionally. And the reactions of those around him had just twisted the knife. The gossip had been painfully humiliating and had just gone to prove to him how little he could count on the people he had thought were his friends. Half the point of moving here was the anonymity the new surroundings afforded.

"All I can say is that, for reasons too complicated to explain, it's the perfect time for me to start over. Move forward, rather. Horse ranching has been a lifelong dream of mine, and I'm finally in a position where I can pursue it. But I'm floundering, here. I'd really like your help to find a viable solution to my problem."

If there was no hotel, no availability at the only B and B and no room for him at Redemption Ranch, then he wasn't sure what that viable solution might be. The only thing he could think of was to find someone willing to rent him a spare bedroom or garage apartment. He hoped it wouldn't come to that. He had more than enough money to make it worth someone's time to rent him the space, but the last thing he wanted to do was to start flinging his money all over town. That was why he'd been so quick to snap up Vivian's offer to borrow her house. He could lay low at the Grainger's, not have to bump heads with any more people than strictly necessary. The less folks knew about him, the better.

People changed when they started figuring out his net worth. He'd seen it over and over again—their eyes filled with dollar signs and any hope he had of establishing a real, personal connection went straight by the wayside. Back in Houston, everybody wanted something from him, and all *he* wanted was for everyone to leave him alone. He could think of nothing better than to hole up on his own little spread of land on the outskirts of Serendipity, where he could fend for himself and not have to deal with cruel and two-faced individuals ever again.

He focused his gaze on her, determination pressing his breath into his throat. "There must be something. Please, Alexis. You're all I've got right now."

Alexis's gorgeous electric-blue eyes widened and her full lips dropped into a pretty little frown that made Griff's gut do a backflip. Alexis was nothing if not gorgeous and he was painfully aware of his own weakness—he was particularly vulnerable to the ladies, beautiful women in particular.

How twisted was that?

In his experience, women were insincere and manipulative. The whole lot of them, bar none. What had he been thinking to have trusted Vivian to be honest with him? He should have known better.

And despite the fact that Alexis had done nothing to make him suspect she might be playing him, he figured it would be smarter to be wary. Better to be safe than to expose a vein. Compassion flooded her gaze and he felt a momentary twinge of guilt that he was pressing her buttons. For a second he was tempted to blurt out the whole sorry truth.

Instead he clenched his jaw until the urge passed. Honesty was overrated. No matter how kind Alexis appeared to be, he knew better than to trust her. Look what had happened when he'd given Vivian a little bit of leeway.

He'd been scammed. Just as with his ex, Caro.

Let Alexis interpret his words any way she wanted. He was here in Serendipity and he wasn't leaving. He shouldn't be penalized because of Vivian—and he wasn't about to let this awkward situation with Alexis force him to tip his hand.

"I understand what you're going through." She was softening toward him—her gaze, her posture, her expression. His expectations rose with the smile on her lips. "Sometimes life changes are—" she paused and gave a little sigh "—seriously complicated."

He wanted to pump his fist in the air. Not that he was necessarily proud of his ability to manipulate people, but he was good at it. And he was winning.

"I'll tell you what. You can stay here at Redemption Ranch as long as you have the need to do so."

Score.

"In the wrangler's bunkhouse, where my ranch hands live."

Or not.

"The *wrangler's bunkhouse?*" he repeated lamely. Surely she was joking.

She nodded.

His lip curled. He'd slept in worse than a bunkhouse—much worse. But that was exactly the point. He was above that kind of lifestyle now. He'd paid his dues and had risen to the top of society. Surely she could see he was too refined to share sleeping space with the hired help. Why, the scarf he was wearing cost more than a rancher made in—

Whoa. How stupid could he be?

His designer clothes were a dead giveaway, suggesting he might be more than a burnt-out shell of a man ready to invest his whole life savings on a ranch. Of course, he'd thought he was going to be alone in the house, so he hadn't given much thought to his choice of attire at the time. But he was thinking about it now— and it mattered, if he was planning to continue in the manner in which he'd originally presented himself: a man of limited means determined to make himself into a rancher. He wondered if she'd noticed his getup, or even if she'd be able to identify the names that accompanied the fancy apparel.

He scoffed inwardly at his own thoughts. What a snob he'd become. The man he'd never wanted to be. At the first available opportunity, he'd visit the general store in town and pick up some plain Western-style clothing so he wouldn't stand out among the natives. If he wanted to *be* a rancher, his attire would be a good place to start. And if it meant that people wouldn't be able to accurately guess his bank balance from his brand names, then all the better.

Luckily for him, she didn't appear to have noticed the high-fashion nature of his clothing, since she was at least partially falling for his *fish-out-of-water* ruse. He sighed in relief.

"Take it or leave it." She slapped her palms on the table with all the finality of a judge's gavel. "It's my best offer. I wish I could do more for you, but I can't."

Griff narrowed his gaze on her, his brow furrowing. She was offering the *bunkhouse* as if it were somehow an answer to prayer.

If Griff believed in the power of prayer—and he didn't—having the opportunity to bunk down with a bunch of rowdy cowhands would not have been what he considered a legitimate answer to his problems. The trouble was, he couldn't think of a better option that wouldn't reveal that he had the means to pay for housing indefinitely, that his bank account was bigger than he was professing it to be.

He leaned forward on his elbows, steepling his fingers under his chin. His mind was spinning, scrambling for a way to salvage this conversation. He'd all but thrown down the gauntlet to her. If he wanted to maintain the slim facade he'd offered, what choice did he have but to accept?

Talk about being caught between a rock and a hard place. And he had no one to blame but himself.

"Okay. Er, thank you for the offer." He flashed what he hoped was a confident grin. "I always wanted to be a cowboy."

She stared at him speculatively, gnawing on her bottom lip.

"What?"

She shook her head. "Nothing."

He suspected he was going to regret accepting her offer. In some ways he already did. If he had a lick of good sense he would just walk out of here right now and *bunk* at the nearest five-star hotel, even if it was an hour's drive away. What he lost in the convenience of the short proximity to the town he could make up in the extravagance of his surroundings.

And why was his heart so set on this particular town, anyway? Surely there were dozens of other places just like Serendipity. Did he really care if he made his home here or somewhere else?

He couldn't entirely explain it, but the answer to that question was yes. He did care where he landed, and this town was it. Vivian had been full of stories about the town of Serendipity and the folks who resided there. According to her, the town was small. Quiet. Unassuming. Becoming a recluse here would be easy, and the surroundings would be peaceful and beautiful. It was a gut feeling more than anything, but he'd learned over the years to follow that internal leading. Why should one small bump in the road cause him to change lanes?

Years before, when the thought first occurred to him that he ought to leave his unfulfilling life in the city and move to a small town to raise horses, he'd simply tucked it into the back of his mind. His subconscious mulled over it, occasionally spearing him with the desire to make that dream a reality. He'd had the means, but he'd been too focused on his career to do anything proactive to make that change.

Then in one painful fell swoop he'd been scammed by a beautiful con artist. Caro had taken what little faith in humankind he'd built up over the years and dashed it against the sharp rock of her conniving schemes. At this point he carried nothing with him but what was left of his shattered heart and the great deal of money he'd made through a career he was no longer interested in pursuing.

He needed Serendipity. He didn't want to find another town. All he had to do was to grit his teeth and get through the next couple of weeks until he found a place to call home, somewhere out of the limelight where he could find rest and peace, where his best friends would be of the equine variety instead of the human kind. He could live with the wranglers. Who knew, they might be able to help him in his quest to launch a ranch of his own. Maybe it was a blessing in disguise.

"You won't be sorry," Alexis assured him with a genuine smile that flooded his senses.

"I'm already sorry," he muttered under his breath, even though he wasn't certain it was true.

Alexis's grin didn't waver, though sparks momentarily filled her eyes. "Don't be. I'm not sure exactly what you're looking for, but I can assure you that you'll be able to pick up some fine property for only pennies on the dollar. You're going to find your perfect home here, I just know it."

Her enthusiasm was contagious. Griff fought to tamp back his excitement, afraid to allow himself to get his hopes up. They'd been dashed so many times before.

"I've saved my whole life for this." That was the absolute truth, though probably not in the way in which Alexis would interpret it. He cleared his throat and broke his gaze away from hers. He didn't want to see his future in her eyes. Not until it was signed, sealed and delivered, in triplicate.

"What made you choose Serendipity?"

Griff chuckled. "Your sister. I'm sure you're aware that she can be quite animated about a subject she's particularly interested in. And persistent, too. She knew I'd been looking for a place in which to settle down and buy a ranch. And she really, *really* loves her hometown. Once she got it in her head that Serendipity was the right location for me to make a place for myself, she wouldn't let up until I agreed to visit."

"She can be pretty persuasive," Alexis agreed with a warm chuckle, but a moment later her brow furrowed and she compressed her full lips. "Sometimes a little too much so. Once she gets an idea into her head, she won't let it go. I apologize on her behalf. She has the distressing tendency to get on a person's last nerve."

Griff raised his eyebrows at her stark admission. "I didn't say that. Your sister is really sweet. A little deceptive, maybe, but I'm sure she was just trying to be helpful."

Or maybe not so much. What had been her plan, sending him out here to the house where her sister lived? She probably had her reasons, but he had no clue what they might be. He was beyond being able to tell, where women were concerned. Whatever. He was here, and that was the point of the matter.

Alexis's lips quirked. "Oh, I'm sure she was trying to help you. The problem is that her idea of 'helping' is focused on what *she* thinks is in the other person's best interest, whether or not the person she's supposedly helping would agree. And she usually pushes the option that helps her the most in the end. I'm sure you've noticed that she can be a little…" She paused and brushed a strand of her long, straight blond hair back behind her ear. "Self-absorbed."

"Really?" Griff struggled not to laugh. In his opinion, all women were self-absorbed. Men, too, for that matter. Always looking out for old number one. And who could blame them? He was no different. "You think she had an ulterior motive for sending me here?"

Had he been played? It kind of felt that way, although he couldn't figure out any legitimate reason for Vivian to have acted deceptively. His mind scoured over the details of his visit. What reason could Vivian possibly have for sending him here, if not primarily to help him find the home he so desired? Viv's boyfriend, Derrick, was the closest thing to a friend Griff had ever had, and they'd both been enthused by the idea.

"You have to admit the circumstances are rather telling," Alexis said, thoughtfully tapping her chin with her index finger. "I don't think it's an accident that Vivian led you to believe I was a guy. She would have had to have been awfully careful not to slip up and refer to me as her sister."

"She used the word twin, not sister. And she called you Alex."

"Well, there you have it, then. She's never called me Alex a day in her life. And then there's the fact that she knew perfectly well I was still living here at the ranch, yet she gave you the impression the house was vacant."

"I'll admit that part sounds a little fishy." And he was beginning to look—and feel—more and more like a sap.

Alexis scoffed. "A little fishy? This whole thing has Vivian's interfering signature all over it."

"Yes, but what could she possibly stand to gain by misleading me?"

"I have no idea." Alexis twirled a strand of her hair around her index finger.

Griff was stumped. And humiliated, to boot. Who knew the internal workings of a woman's mind? He certainly didn't. But the latent anger that was never far from the surface was starting to billow in his chest.

He was *so* over being manipulated. By *anybody*.

"You think we should ask her?"

"Oh, I'm going to ask her," she assured him with a robust nod. She sounded as though she wasn't too thrilled with Vivian's actions, either. "Just as soon as I've got you settled in at the bunkhouse. And we should probably see about getting a new breakfast fixed up here. I think I've got some more bacon in the freezer. It shouldn't take too long to defrost it."

Griff forced a chuckle. "Yeah. My attempt at cooking turned out to be a bit of a disaster, didn't it?"

"I'm sure the dogs appreciated it."

He twisted his lips into a semblance of a smile. "No doubt."

Alexis glanced at the digital clock on the microwave. "Oh, dear. I didn't realize how late it was. It's already a quarter past eight and here I am still in my—" She glanced down at her fluffy purplish-pink robe and her face turned the same color as the material. She was bundled from neck to ankle, but that didn't stop her from gathering the sides of the robe under her chin— the same chin that tipped upward a moment later, set with determination and maybe just a little bit of pride. "I'm afraid I don't have time to cook us a full breakfast. Will a muffin do? I think I've got chocolate chip and blueberry in the breadbox."

Still clutching her bathrobe with quivering fingers, she jerked to her feet and bobbed toward the counter.

"Blueberry will be fine. Are you going somewhere?" He couldn't help but be amused by her stuttering movements. She appeared to be embarrassed about something, and for some reason that put Griff more at ease. Perhaps because it put them on a more equal footing. He knew what it was like to feel uncomfortable. He'd been feeling that way since the moment Alexis had confronted him with her curling iron.

"It's Sunday," Alexis explained. "I have to teach Sunday school to a bunch of middle-schoolers in an hour, and the worship service is right after. Oh!" She turned to face him, her eyes wide. "I'm sorry. I didn't even think to ask you. Would you like to join me? You are welcome to come visit our community chapel, especially since you're planning to move into town. It's probably nothing like the church services you're used to in Houston, but most of the town attends, so you'll have a chance to meet your new neighbors. We're small, but faithful." Her words poured over each other like a waterfall.

Griff barely suppressed the chill that impaled him. Ice entered his lungs, making them burn with the effort of drawing a breath.

He didn't know what was worse—the thought of being surrounded by a town full of people—or the idea that they were all worshipping God. While these folks would be strangers who wouldn't know his painful and humiliating history, he was convinced they'd be quick to draw unsolicited conclusions about him, and Griff had long ago given up on believing any kind of deity existed. Not in his black hole of a world.

"No." He barked the word out more sharply than he should have.

Alexis's jaw dropped and her startled gaze pierced him.

Griff shrugged, backpedaling. "I mean, no thank you. I drove most of the night to get here. If you don't mind, I'd rather just find my bunk and get some shut-eye."

Surprise turned to compassion. "Of course. You must be exhausted. Let me get you a muffin and some orange juice and then I'll show you where you'll be staying. You can visit the chapel another time."

That wasn't going to happen—ever—but for now, Griff allowed Alexis to fuss over him and get him settled in. There was enough time later for him to set her straight on what he was—and wasn't—planning to do during his stay at Redemption Ranch.

Chapter Two

"Are you completely insane? You sent Griff here to do *what?*" Alexis gripped her cell phone close to her ear, glad she was near a chair, because her legs suddenly felt too wobbly to hold her on her feet. She slumped onto the plush burgundy fabric of the recliner and tucked her knees underneath her, coaching herself to slow her rapid, shallow breathing. She was hyperventilating and the room was spinning.

Where was a paper bag when a woman needed one?

"Now, Alexis, calm down." Viv's saccharine voice on the other end of the line sounded as patronizing as it was amused.

"Calm down? You want me to *calm down?*" Alexis was squawking like a parrot and she knew it, but how else was she supposed to react? "You lied to a man who you claim is your friend to send him here, then gave me no warning before waking up to find a strange man in my kitchen while he found a crazy woman in what he was under the impression was a vacant house, and you want me to *calm down?*"

"Well, when you put it that way." Vivian sniffed.

Alexis took another deep breath and prayed for a semblance of self-control. It was a good thing for Vivian that she was in a different city and not in the same room or Alexis might have throttled her.

What a way to ruin a Sunday afternoon. Her spirit had been so calm after spending her morning worshiping the Lord at the chapel. Now any lingering sense of peace she'd experienced had been blown to smithereens.

"You purposefully mislead Griff to get him here, and I want to know why."

"I would never do anything to hurt Griff," Vivian protested resolutely. "He's Derrick's best friend, and that makes him my friend, too."

"All the more reason for you to be straight with him. This doesn't make any sense. Tell me what's really going on."

"I don't know why you're getting so down on me." Viv's voice was close to a whine. "Griff is one of the best-looking men I know."

Alexis knew Vivian's response made perfect sense—to Vivian. Not so much for Alexis, although she privately agreed with her sister's assessment of Griff. He *was* the kind of man that would cause a woman to do a double-take if she passed him on the street. But, honestly, Griff's good looks had absolutely nothing to do with the current situation, except maybe in Vivian's mind—and trying to unravel that mess would be akin to untangling a rat's nest.

"So he's gorgeous. What does that have to do with anything?"

"Oh, you *did* notice, then."

"Vivian," Alexis warned, thoroughly exasperated and very much on the verge of blowing a gasket.

"I'm just sayin'."

"Saying *what?*" Just once in her life, Alexis wished Vivian would connect the dots and make a logical picture.

"I'm sure you've noticed how refined he is. Rich, too."

Refined, yes. Rich? Maybe Griff hadn't said so in so many words, but he'd definitely suggested that he was pinching pennies—something with which Alexis was all too familiar. He hadn't corrected her assumptions, at any rate.

And why did the size of Griff's bank account matter, anyway?

It sounded as if Vivian was trying to set her up—as in matchmaking. Only in Vivian's outlandish fairy-tale mind could a relationship between Alexis and Griff be even remotely possible. Honestly, *any* romantic relationship seemed out of Alexis's grasp most of the time. No matter how many dates she went on, or how many times she got her hopes up, every attempt to find real love fizzled out into nothing. She was the girl a guy dated, not the one he put a ring on. And after kissing so many toads, she was taking an extended vacation from searching for a prince.

Alexis ignored the little twinges in her stomach, writing them off as feeling sorry for having to let her sister's plans down. It wasn't the first time Vivian had come up with a harebrained scheme and somehow involved Alexis in it, but this situation went above and beyond, even for her. Poor Vivian would be in for a shock to discover her fantasy future brother-in-law was actually dirt-poor and world-weary.

"I hate to have to be the one to break it to you, hon, but I don't think Griff is rolling in dough." The man's net worth meant nothing to Alexis, but she knew a thick pocketbook was near the top of Vivian's most-wanted list and therefore—in Vivian's mind, at least—a necessity for Alexis.

Viv burst into giggles. "Did he tell you that?"

"Yes." Alexis frowned, thinking back to her conversation with Griff. He *had* said he was strapped for funds, hadn't he? Or had she put those words into his mouth? Either way, he hadn't contradicted her.

"He's pulling your leg, then, hon," Vivian informed her in a know-it-all voice. "The man has money. Lots of it."

Even though Vivian couldn't see her, Alexis rolled her eyes. "And you know this because…?"

"Did he tell you what he does for a living? He's a venture capitalist. A successful one, too. Trust me on this, Alexis. He's loaded."

Alexis frowned. So Griff was a successful businessman. That didn't explain why Vivian had purposefully deceived him into coming to Serendipity, or why she thought Griff would have any interest whatsoever in her. "I still don't see what that has to do with me."

Vivian tittered. "I should think that would be obvious."

It was. Patently obvious, unfortunately, though Alexis had secretly hoped she'd somehow mistaken Vivian's purpose. "If this is some kind of cockeyed matchmaking scheme, you can forget about it right now."

"You're welcome."

"So let me get this straight. You sent Griff here so I could meet him?"

"Well, I didn't do it for my own good. Let's review his résumé. Handsome. Rich. Sophisticated. What's not to like?"

That was Vivian's short list, not Alexis's. She wasn't even in the market for a relationship anymore. Redemption Ranch, her flailing ministry to troubled teenagers, took every second of her time and energy as it was. Who had time to pursue dating, never mind the time and energy for anything resembling a true relationship? But if she *was* looking—and that was a very big if—her list would read more like "a gentle, down-home cowboy who likes quiet nights at home and working outside with the horses. Those not in current possession of old scuffed boots and worn-out blue jeans need not apply."

In other words, the complete opposite of refined businessman Griffin Haddon with his fancy scarves and designer jeans and spit-shined boots. Of all the brainless, clueless, *obnoxious* shenanigans her sister had ever pulled, this one took the prize.

"Vivian, you can't just jerk people's lives around this way," she reprimanded, feeling like the more mature of the twins, even though she was only older than Vivian by mere minutes. "You sent Griff here under false pretenses!"

"Did not. He really is looking for land. I was trying to be nice," Vivian explained, her voice taking on the hint of a whine. "I felt sorry for the poor man, okay? He recently got his heart broken. We're talking epic crash and burn here. Like, so bad that he started talking about walking away from everything he's built for himself—and he doesn't really want to do that! He's built himself a virtual empire here."

Alexis hadn't experienced that kind of major heartbreak, but she knew how it felt to have the urge to run away from her problems—as fast and far as possible. She could hardly blame the man for deciding to leave if he had the wherewithal to do so. Vivian leaned toward the overdramatic, but Alexis found her curiosity growing nonetheless. "Go on."

"He needs to find somewhere to nurse his wounds and get back on his feet. I thought Serendipity would be perfect for him."

"And so it may be," she agreed. "I understand he's looking to acquire a ranch?"

"Well, he thinks he is. Have you seen him talk about it? His eyes light up like a kid's at Christmas."

"What do you mean, he *thinks* he is? From what I could see, he seemed pretty determined to work his new plans."

"Right now, maybe. Once he's been in Serendipity for a week he'll be bored out of his mind. He's a serious type-A personality. He never sits still. So the slow pace of the town will drive him batty."

"How do I fit into this, again? You don't want me to help him look for a ranch? I thought that's why you sent him here."

"Oh—help him. Do. In fact, it would be really great if you could immerse him in some of the work around Redemption Ranch. A horse ranch is something he's dreamed about since he was a kid. He has no idea what he's truly in for. You should show him what a cowboy really does all day."

"I suppose I could do that." Alexis did know a lot

about ranching—enough to know Griff wasn't precisely what she would consider to be cut out for it. If she didn't miss her guess, once he saw how difficult and physically demanding country work really was, he'd go running back to the city faster than he could say the name of his favorite designer. "Ranching isn't the sort of thing a guy just decides one day that he's going to do. Most of us are raised to be ranchers."

"Exactly. He'll see what dirty work it is and come running back to Houston—back to his *real* career."

She could tell Vivian's concern for Griff was genuine, but there was still a lot that didn't make sense. The whole thing still felt to Alexis like subterfuge. If the whole point was to get Griff to return to Houston, it seemed to Alexis that it would make more sense to let him flounder without any help whatsoever.

Why did Vivian need Griff to return to Houston?

Alexis needed better answers if she was going to be any part of this scheme. She'd have to take valuable time away from her struggling ministry to lend Griff the assistance Vivian apparently thought was a necessary part of the equation. It wasn't that Alexis was being selfish, exactly, but she needed every spare second to try to come up with solutions to her *own* problems, not spend all of her time trying to fix someone else's—especially if the end result wasn't to help Griff obtain a ranch, but rather for him to realize what a pipe dream the whole idea was.

"Why didn't you just call and tell me about your plans with Griff? At the very least, don't you think you should have warned me that he was coming? I could have made arrangements for him to stay somewhere…" She paused and swept in a breath, shaking her head against the cobwebs that were forming. "Else," she finished lamely.

Total silence on the other end of the line. Vivian was many things, but never silent, which nudged Alexis's suspicions to the surface.

"Viv?"

"You aren't going to be mean to him, are you?"

Even though Vivian couldn't see the gesture, Alexis rolled her eyes. "Of course not. When have I ever been mean to anybody? But I have to say you've put both Griff and me into a difficult dilemma, and frankly, I want to know why. There's something you're not sharing with me. Why is it you're so concerned about whether or not I'm being *nice* to Griff? Come clean, sister."

"Just promise me you're going to treat him with extra-special attention."

"What's that supposed to mean? What kind of special attention?" This did not sound good.

"The kind that will be good for both of you! I'm not just doing this for him, you know. Hello! You're a*lone.* You should pop your head into the real world once in a while. You don't take care of yourself, you work too hard, and you don't have enough fun in your life anymore. Play hooky once in a while. Go out to dinner with a guy. With Griff. You know what I mean?"

"Viv! Enough with the matchmaking, already." Alexis was going to protest further, but Vivian had a point, however poorly made. "Okay. Okay. I'll admit I've got a full schedule with the ranch and the kids, but—"

"When was the last time you went out?" Vivian asked, interrupting her. "On a date? With a man?"

"I know what a date is." She sighed in exasperation. "And as a matter of fact, I'll have you know that I—" Her sentence sputtered to a stop.

Uh, oh. Now that she thought about it, it *had* been a long time since she'd been out on a date, official or otherwise. With her two best friends Samantha and Mary happily married and busy with their new husbands, Alexis had pretty much shifted her social life to the back burner. Sure, she attended church and community events just as she'd always done, but she'd never needed a date to do that.

"Exactly!" Vivian crowed, obviously thrilled to have proved her point. "You don't take care of yourself, so it is my solemn duty as your twin to do it for you. What are sisters for, if not that? If I'd told you he was coming, you'd have shuffled him off on to someone else. This way, you *have* to spend time with him—and realize how perfect the two of you are for each other."

"You said the guy is fresh off a heartbreak," Alexis pointed out, propping her hand on her hip. "I doubt he's going to be looking for a new relationship anytime soon."

"Maybe not right away. But once he sees how sweet and special you are, that's bound to change."

"I highly doubt *sweet* is the first word that comes to mind when he thinks of me."

"What? Why? What did you do?" Viv's voice rose and tightened. "You didn't kick him out of the house, did you? Please tell me you didn't."

Alexis groaned. "Not exactly. Well, kind of. He's going to be staying in the bunkhouse with the ranch hands."

"You *didn't!*" Viv wailed.

Alexis's face was on fire. She felt as though she needed to dunk her head in a bucket of ice water to cool down. Why was her sister putting her on the spot this way, as if she was the villain in this melodrama? She'd been thrust into the scene with no advance notice and no lines. How was that fair?

"What else was I supposed to do with him?" she demanded. "Did you really think I'd let some man—a stranger, no less—just move into the house with me? It's not as if I had any warning that he was coming so I would have had time to make proper arrangements." She couldn't help but add that little thrust of the knife, although she doubted Vivian picked up on it.

"You be nice to him. It's important. You've got to win him over." Vivian's voice took on a desperate edge.

"For the last time, Viv, I *am* being nice. I didn't kick him to the curb as I could have done—or worse yet, call the cops on him and have him arrested for trespassing."

Vivian's breath caught audibly. "You wouldn't."

"Of course not, although it could very easily have gone down that way. I can't imagine what you were thinking, sending him to town without giving me a heads-up. I thought he'd broken into our house. He scared me half to death, showing up at the crack of dawn with no warning."

"Oh. I hadn't thought of that."

Of course she hadn't. Vivian rarely thought things through.

"But he's there now and he's staying, right?"

"Yes, he's staying." In the bunkhouse.

"And you'll see to it that he's taken care of? You'll make sure he feels welcome?"

"*Yes,* Viv, I'll look after him while he's here."

"Good, that's good. Be friendly. Talk to him. Get him to talk to you. You're good at that, and he needs it—he's been doing the hermit thing lately. Oh, but you can't tell him any of what I told you." Vivian's voice dropped to a dramatic whisper. "He was completely humiliated by the way Caro treated him, and I'm pretty sure he doesn't want anyone to know about it."

"I promise. Give me a little credit for being sensitive to other people's pain." Alexis didn't care to speculate on Griff's problems. So he had issues. Everyone had some skeletons in their closets. If Griff wanted to keep secrets, she wouldn't interfere.

But didn't he realize she would find him out? At least that he was well-to-do, if not all about his recent heartbreak. Not that she was trying to meddle in his personal life, but one phone call to Vivian and she knew more than she ever wanted to know about Griff Haddon.

Alexis sighed and pinched the bridge of her nose. What difference did it make, anyway? Rich Griff, poor Griff, acts like a beggar man and mistaken for a thief.

"I think you should just roll with it."

"Meaning?" Vivian interrupted her thoughts and she had no idea to what her sister was referring.

"Let him come clean in his own time. I'm sure he'll open up to you, given the chance. Just don't push him away. Please. For me."

Ah, now here it was. "For you? What's in it for you?"

Vivian paused, and it was a long one, enough to shoot Alexis's suspicions into the stratosphere.

"I think I might have mentioned he's a venture capitalist."

"I believe your exact words were that he *was* a venture capitalist, past tense—who, if I'm not mistaken, now wants to leave all that behind and raise horses. And this has *what* to do with you?"

"I can't believe he wants to give up his old life," Viv said. "Not really. He's just hurting right now. He's confused. He does too much good in the community for him to walk away from it all. You should see it. He believes in people when no one else will give them a chance. He helps new small businesses get the financing they need to succeed."

"That sounds like a great career path," Alexis admitted. "And if he's done that well for himself, maybe you're right. Maybe he won't really want to walk away for good, not after he's had time to think things through. You think this might be a lark on his part?"

All the more reason for Alexis not to waste her time with him. If the guy was going to head straight back for the city in a week—forget it.

Vivian scoffed. "Everything was going right for him until that wicked, ruthless woman messed with his head. He was going to help me launch Viv's Vitality. He promised he could get the financing set up for me, and now he's reneging on our agreement. He says he doesn't want anything to do with business anymore. He just wants to get away. Permanently."

Finally the truth had come out. Now everything Viv had done was beginning to make sense. "I'm really sorry to hear that, Viv, but I don't see how your sending him to me is going to help you secure funding for that spa you've been planning. At best, I might be able to steer him toward the purchase of a ranch, but that's the exact opposite of what you want him to do, right? So what are you really asking me for?"

"You can restore his faith in womankind."

Viv's statement was so unexpected—and so outrageous—that Alexis burst into laughter.

"Don't snicker at me. It could happen."

"No, it really couldn't." Vivian had her head in the clouds if she thought Alexis had the time or inclination to romance a city guy with a broken heart even if he'd give her a second glance—which she doubted. And how would that help, anyway?

Vivian sniffled a couple of times. Was she crying?

Oh, brother. Alexis sighed deeply, but her heart was touched nonetheless. The lengths she had to go to for her twin.

"All right," she consoled, her heart tugging with compassion. "Don't cry, Viv. I'm not going to throw myself at the guy, but maybe there's something I can do."

Viv sniffed once more for good measure and Alexis stifled a chuckle. Her sister was such a drama queen.

"You'll back me up, then?"

"I'll try. But I can't promise you this isn't going to backfire. Since at least on the surface it appears Griff is serious about settling down in Serendipity, I'll do what I can to help him secure a place. Maybe he'll realize what a pipe dream he's conjured up and decide to go back to his old life. If the circumstance presents itself, I'll even put a bug in his ear about how great your business plan is and how appreciative you'd be of his assistance. Maybe he'll be willing to help you out once he's had a little time away from the rat race, especially since he promised to help you build your business before all the bad stuff went down. But all the hearts and flowers you imagine will happen between us?" Alexis shook her head. "Let's just be clear about that part right now. Not gonna happen."

Settling into the bunkhouse wasn't as bad as Griff had thought it might be. In fact, to his pleasant surprise, he found it was rather peaceful living next to the barn. Honestly, he had imagined rows of bunk beds with scratchy wool blankets and no privacy among the wranglers, but everyone had separate, if tiny, living quarters, and it turned out that the cowboys were a quiet bunch, mostly keeping to their own devices, which suited Griff just fine. Better yet, the whole place was permeated with the smell of horses and hay, a strong, earthy scent that reminded Griff of the only happy times he'd experienced in his youth.

He discovered he could adapt quite well to this living situation, but then again, adapting was what he'd spent his whole life doing. He didn't know why he should be surprised that this was so easy for him. He was finally here, pursuing his dreams, even if the string of events that had led him to Serendipity was anything but ideal, and even if his plan hadn't gone remotely as he'd expected.

So he'd hit a few bumps in the road—such as finding out the house where he'd intended to stay was otherwise occupied, or when he'd been pawned off to the bunkhouse with one flick of Alexis's pretty wrist. Alexis was definitely the biggest challenge of all. It wasn't every day a man was called out by a beautiful, feisty woman brandishing a curling iron as her only weapon.

It was an adventure, if nothing else, and he was ready for new experiences. Somehow, some way, he was going to find his perfect hideaway out here in Nowhere, Texas. This place was as far away from the world he was used to as a man could get, with horses and open land everywhere he looked. It fit the bill exactly.

His own private haven.

His team in Houston thought he was crazy for wanting to find a home in a small town, but he didn't care what anyone thought about his intentions, even Derrick Reynolds, his best friend and the one and only man he trusted. Griff was tired of living up—or down—to other people's expectations. This was about him and nobody else, and what he really wanted in his life was solitude.

"Griff?" He heard Alexis's raised voice at the same time as her knock—three short, rhythmical raps on the outer bunkhouse door.

"One second," he called, dashing down the hallway to the shared bathroom with his styling paste clenched in his hand. He was dressed in an older pair of blue jeans and a high-end, navy-blue T-shirt. It was the best he could do under the circumstances. He'd planned to buy a few Western shirts at the general store in town, but to his dismay, he'd discovered that the whole town closed up on Sundays. Talk about peculiar small-town culture. He couldn't even get a bite to eat at the local café, much less pick up the groceries he'd intended to buy.

Fortunately for him, he'd had his loaf of bread from the night before. Not only that, but the cowboys had realized his predicament and had graciously offered him the use of their pantry. Otherwise he probably would have gone hungry—or he'd have had to go begging to

Alexis, which he wasn't inclined to do. Thanks to Vivian, he was already beholden to Alexis, more than he wanted to be. He disliked owing anybody anything. He'd rather starve.

He made a mental note to anonymously restock the wranglers' pantry—and maybe add a little bit more variety to their scant offering. They seemed woefully lacking in diversity. How many cans of baked beans could a man eat?

"Griff?" Alexis sounded impatient.

"One second," he called again, dipping his fingers into the pomade and randomly dabbing the paste into his hair. He wasn't a vain man, but his thick hair was downright scary in the morning before his shower. He did the best he could to tame the ragged peaks, then strode to the door.

Alexis's eyes widened as she surveyed him. "I'm sorry if I woke you."

Griff cringed. Apparently he hadn't been entirely successful with the hair.

"No, I was awake. I was reading. Did you need something?"

Alexis's fair skin coloring gave away even the smallest nuances of a blush, and right now her cheeks were rose-petal pink, though he couldn't imagine what she had to be embarrassed about. He leaned his shoulder against the door frame and waited for her reply, which seemed a little bit too long in coming.

It was a simple question, requiring a simple answer. Obviously she needed something or she wouldn't be here knocking at his door. So why was she hesitating? And blushing?

"Well, this is awkward," she muttered.

He raised a brow. "Really? How so?"

"My sister—" She started but then stammered to a stop. She shook her head. "No, never mind. My problem. I'll deal."

What was the woman chattering on about? He waited, hoping she'd finish her sentence. What had Vivian done now?

"It doesn't matter," she continued. "I didn't come here for that."

It would help him tremendously if he knew what "that" was, if he had any expectation of contributing to this conversation. He had to admit he was curious, but it was all he could do to follow Alexis's wild roller-coaster of a monologue.

"I've scheduled a superbusy afternoon ahead of me, so I wanted to make sure I got down here this morning to ask if you'd care to take supper with me."

"Tonight?"

She looked surprised. "No. Well, I mean, yes, but not just tonight. I meant always, while you're here. You're welcome to eat supper at the house every night for as long as you'll be staying on at the ranch, or whenever you're available, anyway. I thought maybe we could spend some time discussing your strategy for finding some land. For starters, I can introduce you to our local Realtor, Marge Thompson."

"There's only one?"

"In Serendipity? Yes—and she only works as a Realtor part-time. She's also our resident insurance agent, so she'll be able to set you up with anything you need for your house and land and car and all that."

"That's convenient," he said, tongue-in-cheek. He swallowed a chuckle. Instead of the soft, lazy Texas drawl that Vivian possessed, Alexis's words were all jammed together and coming a mile a minute, increasing speed at every intersection.

Again he had the impression something was off about her. She was acting skittish. Was she nervous about something?

He was good at reading people, but Alexis had him stumped. Every time he started to believe he had her figured out, she changed. She was a total mystery to him.

Had he said or done something to send her off-kilter? And if he had, what could he do to take the edge off?

"I'd be happy to accept."

Not *that*. He wanted to kick himself for his sheer stupidity. Open wide, mouth, 'cause he had two feet coming.

If only he could take back the words. In his rush to make her feel more comfortable, he'd dived right off the side of a cliff without looking to see if there was water at the bottom of the canyon, never mind how deep. What had happened to his not wanting to be beholden to her? Sharing meals with her was just exactly the kind of thing he was trying to avoid. Here he went again, acting like an imbecile over a pretty face. He'd wanted to ease her obvious discomfort, he'd panicked, and he had blurted out the first solution that had come into his mind. *Idiot*.

"Oh, my goodness," Alexis exclaimed, clapping a palm against her cheek. "I didn't realize. I should have been thinking of your predicament yesterday. I'm so sorry. I didn't think things through. I hope you got along okay last night. You didn't have a thing to eat. Oh, my goodness," she repeated.

He couldn't help but chuckle at how flustered she'd become over his "predicament," as she'd called it. "Don't worry about me. You don't need to feel obligated. I managed just fine. I had supper with the ranch hands. Since the cook has Sundays off, they were kind enough to open a can of beans for me. Oh, and don't forget I had my loaf of bread from breakfast." He grinned, hoping the statement didn't come out sounding facetious. He didn't want to hurt her feelings.

"I am so sorry."

She was an astute woman and correctly interpreted his tone. "No worries. I'll admit it was a bit of a challenge at the outset. I didn't expect all the stores and restaurants in town to be closed on Sunday. But as I said—no worries. It all worked out in the wash."

"But still—I should have realized you'd be in a pinch. I should have at least thought about it. Please forgive me for not realizing your dilemma."

"Not your problem," he reminded her again. "It isn't up to you to make sure I get fed."

As sweet as the woman was for wanting to look out for him, she took too much on herself. He'd showed up out of nowhere with no advance warning, and yet she was treating him as though he was a guest at her ranch. He didn't want her to think she was accountable for him—not in any way, shape or form.

"It kind of is my problem." She propped her fists on her hips, tilted her head up to meet his eyes and set her jaw. Her gaze was no-nonsense, almost daring him to argue with her. She was nothing if not determined.

"You are my responsibility as long as you're staying at my ranch."

No. This wasn't right at all.

It was as if she'd dropped a cage over him, trapping him behind steel bars. He didn't like the feeling. Every muscle in his body tensed for flight and he had to consciously breathe through the urge to sprint away. "Let me reiterate—you are under no obligation to take care of me. I don't want to be any kind of bother to you. I'll just stay out of your way."

And you stay out of mine, he added silently. He'd come out here to get away from debts and commitments. If she took charge of him while he stayed at the ranch, then he would feel beholden toward her, which was the last thing he wanted.

"But you'll still take supper at the house, right? At least tonight? Then you can decide if you want to come back for another meal. I promise not to poison you." She chuckled dryly.

It wasn't the possibility of being poisoned that he was worried about. On the second pass, conceding to her wishes didn't sound any better than it had at first. She was practically forcing him into her debt and he was definitely making extra work for her. He desperately wanted to backpedal, except that her voice sounded so hopeful, not to mention the expectant look in her compelling blue eyes that tugged at his heart despite his best efforts to ignore it.

Those pink-tinged cheeks and that ready smile were hard to say no to. He just wasn't strong enough to deny her.

"I'll be prompt," he promised her through gritted teeth. He was crazy to be doing this. Out of his mind.

She sighed in relief, as if the fate of the world had turned on his answer.

"Great. I'll see you tonight, then," she affirmed cheerfully. "Seven o'clock sharp. Dress is casual. Don't forget. We'll be expecting you."

She didn't wait for his reply. Instead she turned on her heel and walked away, down the porch stairs and back up the slight incline toward the main house.

"Uh—thank you," he called after her, feeling as though he needed to say something nice to her, even if he felt like cursing on the inside. He was digging himself further and further into a hole of his own making.

Wait—what? She'd said *we*. Had she invited others to take supper with her? It seemed like something Alexis would do—try to introduce him to others in the town.

He sighed. Yet another bump in the road. He was trying to avoid people, not engage with them. But Alexis wasn't "people." She was a thoughtful, sensitive woman and even though he knew he shouldn't, he found himself looking forward to sharing supper with her.

He liked her. He wanted to get to know her better.

That made him a fool. And, worse yet, it made Alexis the biggest threat of all.

Chapter Three

Alexis set an enormous platter of home-fried potatoes at one end of the long, rectangular oak dining table and then glanced at her watch. Ten minutes until seven. She had six troubled teenagers fresh off of the bus and joining her for supper tonight.

And then there was Griff.

Her pulse gave a little leap, but she wrote that off to the adrenaline-packed afternoon she'd just experienced. Intake days were always exciting for her whenever she took in a whole new group of kids at Redemption Ranch. Six brand-new hearts to influence with the love of Christ. No matter how surly and offputting they generally acted about it at first, she knew that's all it was—an act. The kids really did crave love, and here at the ranch, that's what they got, in spades.

Showering them with affection was a great part of her theory behind helping troubled kids turn their lives around, although in practice, it was the *tough* part of the love that usually brought about immediate change. She had to show them they mattered to her so they could gain the confidence to believe in themselves.

It wasn't an easy job, and definitely not for the faint of heart. The teenagers pressed her and pushed her to see how far she'd bend. But her methods worked. Her kids didn't leave with the same bad attitudes they arrived with.

And she loved it. She loved the teenagers. In fact, the whole process was a blessing to her. She'd proved herself and her techniques repeatedly in the years since she'd opened Redemption Ranch as an alternative to community service for non-violent juvenile offenders.

Her brain-child. Her ministry.

Her *life*.

Working with teens on this ranch was the only thing she could imagine herself doing with her life; the one career into which she really believed she could put her whole heart.

She reached for a pair of green-apple pot holders and removed the spiral ham from the oven, placing it on the countertop to cool. She smoothed her hair back and sighed, lifting her heart in prayer before her emotions bottomed out. It wouldn't do for the kids, or for Griff for that matter, to walk in and catch her crying.

She didn't have a depressive nature by any means. But at the moment the future loomed black for her. All her hard work at the ranch was going to be for nothing unless God somehow blessed her in a big way with the means to stay financially afloat. And soon.

She hadn't shared her anxieties with anyone. She wasn't the type of woman to burden anyone else with facts she could not change—not even her two best friends Samantha and Mary. No sense worrying them. But the truth was, though the Lord was blessing the ministry in the sense that the teenagers in her care were growing and flourishing both emotionally and spiritually, financially speaking, Redemption Ranch was tanking. She had enough money left—barely—to fund the necessities for this group of kids, but then it was over. Done. Kaput.

Not only was she going to lose her ministry, she was going to lose the ranch if she couldn't find a way to get more money. She certainly couldn't borrow any more. The ranch was already double-mortgaged as it was. How else would she have paid for Vivian's dream to go to cosmetology school in Houston? It had seemed like the logical solution at the time, and with the money she'd gotten from the bank, she'd had a little extra to put into the beginning of her work in ministry.

She had a little income flowing in from the fees the teenagers' parents paid to send them to the ranch as an alternative to community service, though that wasn't nearly enough to cover running such a complex operation. On its own, her relatively small working ranch barely paid for itself between the overhead and salaries. Her ministry went far above and beyond that. The Lord had provided generous ministry partners to support her—at least until the economy crashed. Now it seemed as though nonprofits in general had to fight for every dime they received, and frankly, she just didn't have the know-how or the wherewithal to reach the benefactors she imagined must be out there somewhere. Plenty of nonprofits had professionals on staff solely to handle grant applications—how could she compete with that? Raising money was simply beyond her scope of expertise, and since she was essentially running the ranch on her own, she had no one else to turn to. And she most certainly didn't have the money to hire someone to work out the finances for her. What was the adage? It takes money to make money…

She wished that wasn't true.

It wasn't so much herself that she worried about, although the idea of losing her childhood home simply broke her heart. It was the teens she wouldn't be able to help. And the counselors and wranglers, whose livelihood depended on Redemption Ranch, who would lose their jobs when she folded.

Oh, if only…

Alexis snorted and shook her head. "If only" was a wasted thought. All she could really do was to do what she was already doing and pray that God would provide new answers for the rest of her problems.

Cup half full, even if it was tipped over and leaking all over the floor.

Two sharp raps on the front door alerted her to Griff's presence. She knew it was Griff since the teens and their counselors would come in through the back— and besides, they weren't due for another ten minutes.

"Smells great," Griff said as he entered, making a big show of sniffing the air and patting his lean stomach appreciatively.

"Spiral ham. Home-fried potatoes. Buttermilk biscuits. Broccoli-cheese casserole. Chocolate cake for dessert."

He whistled. "The works! I appreciate it, I mean my mouth is watering here, but seriously, you didn't have to go all out cooking a huge supper on my account," he chided, his voice low and rich.

Her gaze widened. "Oh, I didn't."

His eyebrows hit his hairline and a smile crept up

one side of his mouth. His gray-blue eyes sparkled mischievously.

Heat rose from the tip of her toes to the top of her head. She wasn't easily flustered, but with Griff it seemed as though she was constantly and repeatedly bringing "open mouth, insert foot" to new heights of grandeur.

"That sounded really bad," she admitted, ending the sentence with an awkward laugh.

Griff chuckled. "You think?"

She laid her palms over her flushed cheeks and groaned. "What I meant to say was that while I'm happy you joined me tonight, the full country dinner I've prepared isn't *only* on account of you, although again, you are quite welcome to be here. It's just that I always cook a big supper on the first night of camp. I like to impress my kids before I start putting them to work and making them earn their keep."

"Your *k-kids?*" he stammered, threading his fingers into the salt-and-pepper tips of his hair. "I guess— I mean, I thought… I assumed—"

"Oh, my," she interrupted with a quivering laugh. She really *had* confused him. "Not my kids as in *my* kids. I'm taking you on a mental roller-coaster ride here, aren't I?"

Griff lifted an eyebrow, but at least there was a spark of amusement in his gaze. Alexis had to restrain the urge to burst into giggles at his transparent bewilderment.

"Why don't you come in and have a seat at the table and I'll try to run down exactly what I do here at Redemption Ranch. I'm sorry, I thought you knew or I wouldn't have blurted it out like that. I take it from the flabbergasted expression on your face that Vivian didn't mention what I do for a living—and the ranch hands didn't say anything, either?"

He shook his head and dropped into the chair at one end of the table. "Vivian didn't even mention you were a female," he reminded her. "So, no, she said nothing at all about your career. And the wranglers aren't big talkers. But given the layout of your holdings, and what with your stable and wranglers and all, I assumed ranching was a pretty good bet."

"And if you were speaking to virtually any of my neighbors, you would be spot-on in your assumptions. I, however, use my land for an entirely different purpose. I think you'll find it interesting."

"Yeah? Let's see if I can guess. You mentioned children. You've got a decent spread of land. Do you run a day care? Maybe a summer camp? A dude ranch for kids or something like that?" He reached for the butter knife by his plate and idly threaded it through his fingers. The shiny silver occasionally caught the light from the chandelier hanging directly above the table and formed radiant patterns across the walls and ceiling.

Alexis chortled. "Definitely in the category of 'or something.' Although to be honest, there are days when I do feel very much like I'm running a day care. Or maybe even a zoo. Trust me when I say teenagers can be every bit as stubborn as toddlers. And don't even get me started on the temper tantrums they sometimes throw at me."

The butter knife Griff had been playing with clattered onto his plate.

"Teenagers?" His voice was laced with distaste.

What was up with that? She hadn't even yet told him these kids were all in trouble with the law.

She frowned at his unexpected outburst. "You've got something against teens?"

His face turned a disturbing shade of red. For a moment he looked as if he was about to speak, but then he pressed his lips into a hard, straight line and broke eye contact with her, his gaze shifting to somewhere over her left shoulder.

"Speak now or forever hold your peace," she cautioned, indignation welling in her chest. "Because in about one minute—"

She didn't get to finish her statement, because the minute she'd warned Griff about turned out to be only a matter of seconds. The din of shuffling feet and shrill voices came through the back door as six stylish, if not yet particularly *practically* dressed, teenaged boys and girls clamored into the house. Two of the young men shouted and jostled each other for a position in the lead. Three girls entered directly behind them, huddling together and effusively giggling at something one of the young ladies was saying. Lagging at the rear was a third boy. His solid black trench coat and military boots matched his shaggy, ink-black-dyed hair. He clearly didn't fit in with his peers, and wasn't even trying to—rather, he was working hard at giving the impression he didn't care. Resentment and bitterness wrapped around him every bit as voluminously as his trench coat. His hooded brown eyes simmered with bad attitude and negativity.

Alexis had seen it all before and it didn't rattle her. This boy was far from the first to arrive at Redemption Ranch angry at the world and with a chip the size of Texas on his shoulder—though unless she found a way to make ends meet, he might be the last.

From the files she'd received on each of the kids, she knew that the boy in black was Devon, an only child, and that he came from a tragic situation. His mother had passed away quite suddenly from cancer and he now lived with his strict, if wealthy and influential, father. From what Alexis could gather, the man did very little for his son, other than provide him with what money could buy. Kids needed so much more than possessions.

Of course, she couldn't be sure without meeting the man, but she had the sense that Devon's father was one of the well-to-do parents who were only too happy to pay to have their child attend the ranch instead of having to perform community service, with or without the attitude adjustment Redemption Ranch offered, not because they wanted what was best for their kid but because they wanted to maintain their own public image. It was easy to make up excuses as to why their kid disappeared for a month, far simpler than taking the chance of someone influential seeing their teenager in an orange vest picking up trash along the side of the highway. The parents' motivations sometimes saddened Alexis, but whatever reasons brought the teens to the ranch, the point was that they were now in a place where they'd finally have people who truly wanted to help and understand them.

That's where Alexis came in. As she'd done with so many boys before him, she had every intention of showering Devon with genuine love and affection and seeing if she could break through the thick barriers he'd constructed around himself.

Behind the kids came two counselors in their early twenties wearing patient, determined looks on their faces. Marcus Ender, the male counselor, immediately spotted Griff sitting at the head of the table and moved to greet him. Tessa Applewhite, the female counselor, grinned and winked at Alexis.

"And the fun begins," Tessa quipped under her breath as she passed.

Alexis chuckled and nodded in agreement, though she wasn't feeling the excitement and enthusiasm she usually did. Wrangling troubled teenagers actually *was* her idea of fun, and she usually enjoyed the first night's dinner and getting to know her new crop of kids. She was used to the teenagers posturing and giving her guff and didn't let it bother her.

It was Griff's attitude that was ruining it for her. Something about his peculiar reaction to the scenario set her on edge. His very presence at her table changed the equation in a way she couldn't comprehend.

She didn't need the extra stress right now. She hadn't even had the opportunity to explain the ministry she performed here at Redemption Ranch, and yet it appeared Griff had already come to his own conclusions about the project—and not very good ones, at that. He sat straight-backed on the edge of his chair as if he had a pike in his spine, and the expression on his face was nothing short of a grimace.

What was rattling him?

It wasn't as if the teenagers were going to bite him. Sure, the kids could get a little rowdy at times, but she'd never allow it escalate to the point of jumping on the table yodeling like Tarzan and beating their chests, for pity's sake.

If Griff didn't like teenagers, he was staying at the wrong ranch. If that was his problem, it would be better for everyone concerned if he figured that out now, she supposed. Should he need to look elsewhere for accommodation, now would be the time.

Vivian's meddling seemed to be creating a great deal more problems than it was solving. Naturally her sister wasn't even in town while all this was transpiring. No, she'd left it up to Alexis.

"Thanks for nothing, Viv," Alexis grumbled under her breath before addressing her erstwhile visitor. "Griff, this is Marcus and Tessa, the teens' counselors. Marcus, Tessa, this is my houseguest, and a friend of Vivian's, Griffin Haddon."

"Houseguest being a relative term," he muttered with a nod to the counselors.

Tessa giggled and shot Alexis an inquiring glance.

"Meaning he's bunking with the wranglers," she offered with a wry twist to her lips. At this point, the man should count himself fortunate that she hadn't tossed him out on his ear. The idea was becoming more and more appealing by the moment.

"Not family, then." Tessa sounded a little bit disappointed, though Alexis couldn't fathom why it mattered whether or not she and Griff were related.

She shifted a speculative gaze to her *houseguest,* who was studiously avoiding looking at anyone, most especially Tessa. His face appeared heated and he was fidgeting with his hands, pulling at the collar of his T-shirt with the tip of his index finger.

Then suddenly it hit her.

Oh. How had she missed something *that* obvious? Alexis was usually right on top of emotional interchanges—especially potentially romantic ones. She was losing her touch if she couldn't see what was happening here.

Tessa was sizing Griff up as a dating prospect. Well, at least that explained why she was interested in the relational status between Griff and Alexis. If Griff was family, then Alexis wasn't potential competition. Tessa was simply trying to make sure she wasn't treading on Alexis's turf.

She snorted softly. Of course Tessa wasn't. If she was interested in Griff then she was welcome to him. Griff was an attractive man, if a lady was interested in well-to-do city guys. Griff was exactly the kind of man Vivian would go for, but he wasn't the type of guy that would cause Alexis's heart to hum.

Nope. She'd never be interested in a man like Griff Haddon, and it appeared he was likewise not concerned—with anyone or anything. He certainly wasn't making any effort to be charming toward Tessa, or even all that polite. His posture was as rigid and solid as a brick wall. If it was possible, he stiffened even further when the teenagers gathered around the table and started taking their seats.

Whatever.

Alexis was done with trying to deal with Griff's problems, never mind trying to figure out his sudden shift in attitude. She was beginning to be sorry she'd even invited him to be part of the dinner, if he was going to act like a jerk about it. She had enough emotions spiraling off the temperamental teenagers who were essentially being forced into a shocking new environment without adding a sulking man to the mix.

Griff was getting in the way of her joy, but she realized that could only happen if she let it—and she wasn't going to let it happen.

"Please be seated, everyone," she announced, moving to the head of the table, which had the unfortunate consequence of placing her directly opposite Griff. She astutely avoided his gaze, choosing instead to capture the teenagers' lax attention with a wave of her arms. She silently rehearsed the teens' names, putting each name with a face. Connor, Josh, Devon, Saralyn, Hailey and Destiny.

Her kids.

"If we could all please join hands, I'd like to thank the Lord for bringing us all together," she announced. The two counselors already had their hands held out palms up, anticipating her request, but seven pairs of eyes stared back at her as if she'd just grown antlers— Griff's the most startled of the bunch.

Alexis lifted an eyebrow and pointedly looked at his hands, which were clenched in front of him, fisted on each side of his plate. He glanced to where her gaze rested and his lips twitched into a frown. Scowling, he looked to his right and then his left, where Marcus was grinning and holding a hand out to him. Alexis watched Griff's gaze turn dark. Was his mind at war on whether or not to make a scene?

She was beyond caring what Griff did or did not choose to do. Instead of pressing the issue, she bowed her head and closed her eyes, her hands still expectantly open to the teenagers sitting on either side of her.

"Heavenly Father, we thank You for this food," she started, not at all surprised when the teens seated beside her belatedly clasped their hands in hers. By and large, these were good kids who just needed a little encouragement in their lives. Which they would get, from her, starting tonight and beginning with a prayer. "And we thank You for the company we have gathered together here now."

Even if very few of those gathered around her table apparently wanted to be *here* at all. She peeked across the table through half-closed lids. All the teens had joined hands. Only Griff had staunchly refused, his gaze narrowed on the plate in front of him and his fists still clenched tightly.

She masked her sigh of exasperation. The man was more difficult than the entire group of teenagers put together, and that was saying a lot. But she was in the middle of addressing the Almighty. She shouldn't be allowing Griff's attitude to affect hers. She continued with her prayer, her voice strong and perhaps a little bit obstinate.

"May Your blessing rest on each of us not only tonight, but throughout these few short weeks we will be together. Through Christ our Lord. Amen."

She grinned at the lukewarm chorus of *amens* that followed. A few weeks in her care and she knew *lukewarm* would advance into *hearty*. This was going to be a wonderful month, she could just feel it. Lives were going to be changed for the better. Griff Haddon's bad attitude wasn't going to ruin this for her—or for them.

"Dig in before the food gets cold!" she urged enthusiastically.

Everyone obliged, with two exceptions—Griff, who leaned back in his chair, folded his arms over his chest and glared at his empty plate, and Devon, who was staring defiantly at the two boys on the other side of the table. Alexis wondered what had gone down between Devon and the other young men before they'd arrived at the dinner table, and made a mental note to ask Marcus about it when they met later on in the evening.

"What are you staring at, emo dude?" Connor challenged, elbowing Josh and jabbing his chin toward Devon. "You got a problem?"

Devon didn't answer, nor did he drop his gaze. Alexis could almost palpably feel the combustible thick tension building across the table. She scrambled for a way to end the standoff before it became ugly and exploded.

"Speak up, Blackie," Josh taunted. "You scared? You want to go running home to your mama?"

Devon stood so quickly his chair tipped over behind him. His eyes turned glassy as he pressed his fists against the table and leaned in toward Connor.

"Don't you ever talk about my mama," he warned through clenched teeth, slamming his fists against the tabletop so hard the dishes rattled.

Josh laughed harshly. "Or what, emo boy?"

"Or you'll answer to me." To Alexis's very great surprise, it wasn't Devon who had responded, or even one of the counselors. The low, calculated words came from Griff's mouth. Everyone's gaze snapped to his.

Alexis had no doubt Griff meant what he'd said. His jaw and shoulders were every bit as tense as Devon's. This wasn't simply about quelling a potential brawl before it started, or lending assistance just because he happened to be sitting at the table when it all broke out.

No—this was personal.

Apparently, Connor and Josh saw the same thing she saw in Griff's gaze, for they immediately backed down and made a big show of laughing it off.

"Whatever, dude. We were just joking with him," Connor said. "It's all cool."

"Right." Griff's voice was deceptively mild.

Devon continued glaring at the two boys across the table as he righted his chair and returned to his seat.

The girls giggled until Griff's gaze narrowed on them and abruptly cut them off. "You have something you want to add?"

It was one thing to put a damper on the testosterone in the room, but quite another to frighten the girls unnecessarily. When it came to female teenagers, their giggling was a nervous gesture more often than not, certainly not intentionally harmful. But the way Griff was glaring at them, Alexis suspected he thought they were ganging up on Devon, whom for some inexplicable reason Griff had elected to champion.

It was time to diffuse the situation before something worse happened, and food, she knew, was her best weapon in the battle.

"Who wants spiral ham? I'm serving. Pass your plates," Alexis announced, waving her serving fork and knife like a conductor in a symphony. "Fresh out of the oven. I glazed it with butter and honey," she tempted. "Devon? You hungry?"

Tension melted as the teens passed their plates. The counselors jumped in with standard-issue, get-to-know-you questions, which everyone reluctantly participated in, with the notable exception of Devon. The surly youth passed his plate with the rest but ate his food in silence without ever lifting his gaze.

It was only after she'd served everyone else that she realized Griff's plate was still empty. Apparently his wasn't one of the plates that had been passed around, and from the look of things, it had been purposefully. He sat stock-still, his arms still crossed, his confrontational gaze locked squarely on her face.

What? He didn't think she'd had enough altercations for one evening?

"Griff? Why don't you pass your plate down to me so I can load you up with some ham?"

He stood abruptly, the feet of his chair scratching against the hardwood floor. "No, I don't think so. I'm sorry. Excuse me."

Without another word, he strode out of the dining room as though his tail was on fire. A moment later she heard the front screen door slam.

Alexis watched him leave, her mouth agape. What had just happened? And just when she'd thought she'd broken the resistance at the table—or most of it, anyway. Men. Honestly. Give her a cranky teenager any day of the week.

"I—I'm sorry," she stammered. "I don't know what to say. You guys go ahead and eat before your food gets cold. I'm, um, going to—" She gestured toward the door instead of finishing her sentence.

She ought to just let him go, she thought as she shot off after him, anger pulsing through her veins. Whatever his problem was, he needed to deal with it. Or at least cool off a bit. But if she waited for that to happen, *she'd* have time to cool off, as well, and quite honestly, she wasn't willing to wait. She wanted to confront him while she was good and angry.

"Griff, wait," she called as she flounced out the front door and down the steps. He was already halfway around the house, presumably headed for the wrangler's bunkhouse. She wasn't sure he was going to acknowledge her, but after she called his name a second time, he stopped and turned, his posture stiff and his jaw tight with strain.

He glowered at her. He clearly wasn't over whatever had set him off.

"Why did you follow me?" he asked.

"Why did you storm out of there?" she countered, propping her fists on her hips and narrowing her gaze on him. "And after all that, you didn't even eat anything."

"I've lost my appetite."

Well, that was rude. Frankly she didn't care much one way or the other if his stomach was empty. It was his own fault he was in this predicament. As far as she was concerned, after the way he'd acted, he could very well starve to death. She wasn't feeling particularly generous at the moment.

"Why?" It was a simple question, and after the scene he'd just put her through, she deserved an honest answer.

He frowned and shoved his hands in the front pockets of his jeans. "I'd rather not talk about it."

So there was something, then. She'd suspected it wasn't just bad manners. But now she was really curious.

"I don't understand."

His gaze narrowed on her, then shifted somewhere over her left shoulder. "There's nothing to understand."

"Really? Because I think there is."

He sighed and it nudged at her heart. She didn't want to feel sorry for him. She didn't want to feel *anything* for him, Vivian and her crazy schemes notwithstanding. Yet something about his expression bade her to continue.

"I'm a good listener," she prodded in a gentler tone of voice. Maybe if she backed off a little he'd be more inclined to share his feelings with her.

"Look, I know you want answers, but my personal business is none of your concern. I'm outta here." He didn't wait for her to press further. Instead he turned on his heel and took long strides toward the side of the house.

"See you tomorrow night for supper?" She didn't know why she asked when the answer was obvious even before his voice drifted back to her.

"I don't think so."

Griff couldn't get out of there fast enough. He'd wanted to scream, or to kick, or to punch something. Nothing he could do in mixed company, especially in front of impressionable children. He certainly hadn't expected Alexis to follow him out of the house and demand answers from him.

He'd told her the truth. There was nothing to say.

When he reached the bunkhouse, he paused at the door and then turned and headed out toward the nearest open field. It was growing dark and he had to tread carefully to keep from losing his footing, but he surged forward, scanning the way in front of him, glad to have something to keep his mind at least partially occupied outside of what had just happened with Alexis and the kids.

He'd started squirming the moment the teenagers had arrived. High school hadn't been a good experience for him, not a second of it, and he had no inclination to relive it through interaction with Alexis's *kids*. But then Devon had walked through the door, all tough and defiant, acting as though he didn't have a care in the world, as if it didn't matter that he was clearly an outcast, different than other kids. Griff had immediately lost the slim grip on his present reality. Devon's hidden vulnerability caught his eyes like a beacon and, despite Griff's best efforts to the contrary, the boy's condition tugged at something deep in his heart.

That kid was him.

Just seeing Devon slumped in his seat avoiding eye contact with everyone, mad at the world and everything in it—it was too much for Griff to handle.

He knew that feeling. He'd lived it. Devon seemed to come from money, which was the polar opposite of Griff's childhood, but the frustration, the isolation—all of that was far too familiar.

It had been all he could do to keep his mind from tunneling back to the past. He had broken into a sweat trying to consciously remind himself that he wasn't a vulnerable teenager anymore. He'd grown beyond needing the acceptance of his peers. He didn't care what anyone thought about him, and he was better off that way. But reminding himself didn't make it any easier to sit by Devon and watch the unhappiness pour off the kid in waves.

Getting out of there? Self-preservation, pure and simple.

At least, that's what he kept telling himself. So why was his conscience niggling at him and not giving him a moment's rest?

Maybe because Alexis had been especially kind and generous to him. She'd extended her hospitality even when she was under no obligation to do so; invited him to be a guest at her table.

And what had he done? Rudely packed up and marched off.

She should have been furious with him for the way he'd stormed off in the middle of a supper she'd clearly spent all day preparing—and maybe she had been, at first. Yet while there was no doubt she was still confused by his behavior, he'd actually read kindness and compassion in her gaze.

How could she find anything in him or this situation to have sympathy for?

His dander rose once again. He didn't want her pity. And he most certainly didn't need her prying into his personal business. He couldn't and wouldn't explain why seeing the teenagers ganging up on Devon had set him off, but he couldn't deny one fact—he did owe Alexis an apology. He wasn't sure exactly what he'd say to her when the time came, but there had to be something he could do to put things to right. He had to try.

A quick glance at his cell phone told him he'd been walking for well over an hour. He hadn't realized how deeply lost in his own musings he'd been. This whole situation had really thrown him for a major loop.

It was time for him to stop feeling sorry for himself and act like a man and not one of those snotty kids Alexis was apparently fond of. Straightening his shoulders, he turned around and took long, purposeful strides toward the house.

By the time he returned to the ranch, Alexis's young guests would hopefully have gone back to wherever it was that they were staying—Griff guessed the two structures located on the opposite side of the main house from where the wranglers bunked.

If the kids were still lingering over supper, he'd hold off and remain outside until he'd seen them leave, but he didn't want to wait until morning to resolve this problem. He'd made up his mind about speaking to Alexis and wasn't the kind of man to put off doing what needed to be done.

Especially when it involved eating crow. In his opinion, the sooner this was over with, the better.

Relief surged through him when he realized the house was dark, which meant the kids had probably moved on. The porch light beckoned, reminding him of the first time he'd seen the place, pulling up in front of what he'd believed was an unoccupied house. Instead, he'd frightened Alexis into confronting him with her curling iron. He chuckled under his breath. She wasn't timid, that one. The fire in her gaze was enough to daunt *this* accidental intruder.

For a moment he debated whether or not to bother her. He opened the porch screen and was about to knock when he realized the door was cracked open. A dim light flickered from a room to the left of the living area.

"Alexis?" he called softly, feeling uncomfortable disturbing the silence. "It's Griff. I need to speak with you. Do you have a second?"

She didn't answer. Maybe she couldn't hear him. He tried again, raising his voice slightly louder. "Alexis? Are you in there?"

"I'm in the office, Griff." Her usually confident and upbeat voice had an odd hitch to it. Curious as to what that meant, he let himself in, following the sound and the light.

Her office was lit only by the fire glowing in the hearth—a real wood fire, not the flip-the-switch gas type he'd had in his apartment in Houston. The whole place smelled of smoke and pine. The room was lined with floor-to-ceiling bookshelves carrying haphazard piles of books boasting ragged spines that had clearly been cracked open, some many times. Scanning the titles, he determined there was no rhyme or reason to the setup. She wasn't flaunting anything. It wasn't about prestige or scholarship or even decor. As with everything else he knew about Alexis, her library was the real thing.

Alexis sat slumped behind her mahogany desk, nearly hidden by the high stacks of paper and ledgers scattered across the desktop. Unlike the rest of her tidy house, her desk looked as though a dog had chased a cat over it. Her forehead was propped on her hand and her face was hidden behind her palm, almost as if she was nursing a headache. When she raised her head, Griff was surprised to find her luminous blue eyes brimming with moisture.

His gut clenched. Was she crying because of him?

Women and tears were a bad mix. Granted, in his experience, the tears were often faked and usually accompanied by whiny demands. But he had absolutely no doubt that the tears in Alexis's eyes were all too sincere. She hadn't been expecting his arrival, so she couldn't possibly have an agenda. In fact, he felt rather as if he'd caught her completely off guard. From the frantic way she dashed the moisture from her cheeks, she wasn't trying to be the least bit manipulative. She didn't even want to acknowledge she was crying.

"I'm sorry," she offered in a soft, sweet soprano voice. Again he noticed the tight, odd hitch in her tone. "I wasn't expecting company. I—"

"Please. Don't apologize to me. I'm the one who should be saying I'm sorry."

"What? Why?" She sounded genuinely perplexed, as if she'd completely forgotten what an oaf he'd been at supper and the confrontation that had followed.

"I can't believe you have to ask," he replied with a low groan. "Look. I didn't mean to interrupt you, and I won't stay. I just stopped by to apologize for how shoddily I acted tonight at supper."

"Oh." Their eyes met and for a moment he forgot to breathe. She didn't look *at* him, she looked *into* him, as if she were able to read the very depths of his soul.

Disconcerted, he broke his gaze away and walked over to the nearest bookshelf, breathing heavily. *Steady, Haddon.*

"You like reading the classics?" he asked, noting *Pride and Prejudice* and *Jane Eyre*.

"I like reading everything," she said, stepping out from behind her desk and moving to his side. She offered him a tentative smile. "As long as it has a happy ending."

"Ah. A romantic at heart," he teased with a low chuckle.

"Guilty as charged."

"I can't say I'm surprised." And he wasn't. Of course Alexis thought in those fanciful terms. Happily ever after. As if that existed. It was all he could do to keep from scoffing aloud. But he couldn't fault her. From what he could gather, she'd led a fairly sheltered existence in this little town. She probably didn't realize how nice she had it, never having had to experience the *not* so happily ever after.

"You sound like you don't believe in happy endings." Her statement could have come out accusatory or condescending, but actually, it sounded as if she pitied him. That was the last thing he wanted.

"Don't feel sorry for me," he said, his shoulders tightening. His voice sounded a little harsher than he'd intended.

"I don't," she assured him. "I just wonder—that is, something must have happened to make you feel that way."

Their gazes met and his skin prickled all over, as though a million fire ants were crawling on him. He strode to the fireplace and picked up the iron poker, jabbing into the largest piece of firewood in the hearth and sending up a shower of sparks.

"When I came in it looked like you were crying. I don't mean to pry, but do you want to talk about what's got you so upset?" he asked. It wasn't his business, and if he had any sense at all he really shouldn't get involved, but he was desperate to turn her attention away from him and the happily-ever-after nonsense, and so he grabbed at the most obvious diversion.

"You really want to know?" She sounded surprised.

As well she should be. But she couldn't be nearly as shocked as *he* was. It was disconcerting to realize he really did want to know what had this beautiful woman so distressed. He should know better than to pry, but there it was again. His Achilles' heel staring right at him. Why did he have so much trouble saying no to a pretty face?

"Well, sure I do. If you want to tell me," he replied, clearing his throat of the low, husky tone.

She sighed and moved to the small green sofa by the fireplace, slinking onto the cushion and pulling her knees up. She gestured to an armchair opposite her. "You may as well sit down. It's a long story."

Even as he seated himself, he wondered at the wisdom of staying. What a fool he was. He knew better than to stick his nose where it didn't belong—and he had a sinking feeling he was about to get in deep. He shouldn't care.

But he did—at least enough to stay. He leaned back in his seat and crossed his legs. "Go on."

She chuckled dryly, but it wasn't a happy sound.

"*Once upon a time…* Or maybe I ought to be starting with *I have a dream…*"

Chapter Four

Alexis was surprised and impressed by Griff's willingness to acknowledge his boorish behavior at the supper table. Not every man was mature enough to admit when he was wrong. But she was even more astounded by the apparent interest he was taking in hearing about her problems. He'd seemed so closed off earlier, not wanting to talk about his own issues, that she hadn't expected him to be so sympathetic to hers.

She shook off the feeling and pressed it behind her. She knew better than to judge a man's outer actions without knowing what was in his heart.

"I'll begin at the beginning," she said, smiling at her handsome and attentive houseguest.

He returned her smile stiffly and leaned back into the cushion, curling his arm across the top of the armchair and inadvertently calling attention to the bulge of his biceps.

Alexis quickly averted her gaze. "As you may have gathered, I minister to troubled teens."

He exhaled sharply. "Hmm. Yeah. I got the 'troubled

teen' part of it, all right. Is that why you were upset when I came in? They giving you *trouble?*"

She chuckled at his attempt at a joke. "The kids? No, not at all."

He raised a brow.

"Well, no more than usual, anyway. This is the first night here for this new batch of teenagers. They have some big adjustments to make. You may not have seen them at their best this evening."

He scoffed. "That's a charitable way of putting it."

"Charitable? No. Give them a couple of weeks. They're here for a full month, what I've termed a Mission Month. They'll be put to work learning the inner workings of ranch life. They just need a little love and something worthwhile to do with their time. Redemption Ranch provides both. And as an added plus, they get so much exercise that they're too tired to bicker with each other."

"I see," he said, but he certainly didn't sound as though he understood what she was trying to say. Or else he didn't believe her.

"For the most part, these kids are just misunderstood."

Griff grunted. There were those rose-colored glasses again. The woman lived in Wonderland, not the real world. He'd watched the interplay over the supper table. What these kids were was *mean.*

She sighed. "I know that to the casual onlooker, they might have come off as being a little harsh tonight."

"You think?" he snapped back before he could temper his response. "They played judge and jury on that kid Devon for no good reason. Just because he looked different from the rest of them. He didn't stand a chance against those 'misunderstood' miscreants.''

"Talk about being both the judge and jury, Griff. You've already pretty much ruled on the case, and without the least bit of evidence."

"Oh, I have evidence." *A past full of it.*

"Enlighten me."

For the briefest of moments he considered unloading his whole sorry story on her, but to his very great relief the feeling passed before it could take root. His whole body stiffened in protest. He wasn't about to *share* his life with her.

"Let's just say I have good reason for feeling the way I do."

"But you liked Devon. Or at least, you felt protective of him. Why?"

The hair prickled on the back of Griff's neck. The woman was observant. Far too much so. He'd have to watch himself around her.

"No reason. I just don't like to see people giving each other trouble. Even if they're just kids. I don't care for mean-spirited teenagers."

"That's rational. But I don't buy that that's the only reason you stuck up for Devon the way you did. There's got to be more to it than that."

Griff shrugged. It was no matter to him what she thought. He was done talking.

"The teenagers will come around," she assured him when he didn't respond. "They always do. A couple of weeks of working together under supervision and they'll start to bond with each other. Before you know it, they'll all be friends. Problem solved."

Enjoy your pipe dreams, lady.

"You seem to have it all worked out," he said aloud.

"I've seen it with my own eyes. Countless times."

She sounded confident. And sincere. But people could be sincerely wrong, and he was convinced this was the case with Alexis. She saw what she wanted to see and believed what she chose to believe. That didn't make what she perceived a reality.

Griff knew better.

"How long have you been doing this…this thing with the kids?"

"I planned and dreamed for a long time before my ministry here at Redemption Ranch came to fruition. For a long time I didn't think it would happen at all," she explained, a faraway look clouding her eyes. "When my grandfather left me and Viv the ranch, the timing finally seemed right to try to make those dreams a reality."

"And so you have."

She wrapped her arms around her legs and propped her chin on her knees. "Mostly, I guess."

"You said you've seen some measure of success with the kids."

"I have. It's just…" Her sentence drifted off.

"Just what?"

She shook her head. "I shouldn't burden you with my problems."

"I'm a good listener. Hit me up." Griff inhaled sharply. The words had left his mouth of their own accord and he couldn't reel them back, no matter how much he wanted to. Why had he even said that? He was a terrible listener—or at least, he was now. It used to be his favorite part of his work as a venture capitalist, listening to people lay out their dreams, talk about what they wanted to achieve and the obstacles that lay in their paths. Then he could swoop in and make it all happen for them. After a childhood that had left him feeling constantly powerless and on the outside, it had been an unending rush to be on the ground floor of so many businesses, helping to make them come together—to make dreams come true.

Then, of course, Caro had happened. Listening to her had been the worst mistake he'd ever made. So he'd decided not to listen anymore. And if he was going to start, it wouldn't be with someone like Alexis, given that he didn't buy what she was saying about her ministry.

Turning teenage delinquents into model citizens? Yeah, right.

And yet…

And yet he believed that *she* believed in what she did. Her whole countenance shined when she spoke about the teenagers in her care.

For the moment that was enough to make him want to reach out to her, even if he didn't personally appreciate what she was trying to do. If nothing else, it would even the score between them. She had helped him, so he would help her.

He moved across the space separating them and took a seat next to her on the couch, draping his arm across the back and laying his other hand atop both of hers, gently prying them apart.

"Talk to me," he urged again, softly yet compellingly. "You were crying when I came in. Why? Your ministry is clearly a success. You have the opportunity to follow your passions—to do what you really want to do with your life. Are you aware of how rare that is? What could be better than that?"

When she laughed, her voice caught on a hiccup. "The *people* part of Redemption Ranch is going great guns. I'm thoroughly confident in the work I do here. But the finances? Not so much. I think I'm going to send my board of directors to early graves."

Finances. Her problem was money. Not emotions. Not people.

Money.

Griff immediately felt the tension from between his shoulder blades ease. He wanted to cheer. Fixing financial dilemmas was a walk in the park for him, and solving money problems was his forte. Perhaps he could advise her.

"You're a nonprofit, I presume?"

"That's one way of putting it." She laughed. "No, seriously. I receive a little bit from the parents of the teenagers for their care while they're here, but not enough to cover my overhead. Most of them could afford to pay more, but I couldn't possibly put the price tag out of reach of families who don't have as much to spare. The expenses are more than I'd anticipated when I started the program. Food, the upkeep of the horses, not to mention the salaries of the wranglers and counselors involved. It really is a ministry, and I was hoping to find benefactors who'd find what I do worthwhile, but honestly, I'm having trouble finding folks to support the cause. I'm not good at advertising. I know nothing about grant writing. And I really hate asking for money. I wouldn't, if I didn't have to."

"You neglected to mention yourself in this equation."

"Me?"

"You've got to pull in a living from this, right? Put food in your own mouth. Buy an occasional new outfit?"

She shrugged. "In theory. When I started out I was using money left over from double-mortgaging the ranch."

"You double-mortgaged your home to invest in your ministry?"

"Not really. My primary purpose was to get Vivian through cosmetology school. There was a little money left over, and I used that. The truth is that recently I've been tapping into my very limited 401k, which I'd built up before I'd started working at the ranch full-time. I just discovered tonight that it's completely drained. I'm done. I've literally poured every cent I have into this ministry, and I have failed at finding a way to keep it going." Her sentence ended with a sob that wrenched Griff's heart.

He chucked her on the chin, forcing her to meet his gaze. "Not yet, you haven't. It sounds to me like all you need is to find some new investors."

"I've tried. But I guess I'm really not any good at asking people for money. At one point I had a few ministry sponsors—I hesitate to call them investors—but most of them have dropped off, what with the economy being what it is. I'm not sure what role I played in the failure, if maybe I wasn't as good as I should have been at providing updates and the like, or I didn't say the right things. The teens take up most of my time, and the paperwork—" She paused and gestured toward her desk. "Well, you can see how behind I am on that mess. Before you say it, hiring a personal assistant is out of the question."

"Right. Back to finances again."

She groaned and scrubbed her palms against her eyes. "The story of my life. Literally. I really hate money."

"I may be able to help you."

She glanced up, her glassy-eyed gaze displaying a shimmer of hope before they dimmed. She nibbled at her bottom lip and shook her head. "I didn't share my story to get something from you. I know you... That is..." She sighed instead of finishing her statement. "I'll figure it out. There must be some way out of this mess. I just need to spend more time on my knees praying about it and to look for God's answers."

Right. God's answers. Because, of course, God had time to listen to the prayers of a simple country girl.

Griff knew better. God was too busy to answer the prayers of mere mortals. How many times had he called out to God as a youth? God hadn't listened then. There was no reason to suppose He would bother now. Alexis was wasting her time.

"God helps those who help themselves," he reminded her.

She chuckled dryly. "That isn't in the Bible, you know."

"It isn't?"

"Nope. I don't know who made that saying up, and I personally wouldn't want to try living my life without knowing I can rely on God's help, no matter what."

Griff's jaw tightened. The only thing that kept him from snapping at her was the fact that she was already upset and he didn't want to make it worse by spouting off his opinions on the subject of divine intervention.

"All I can do is keep doing what I do best, which is work with the teenagers, and let God handle the rest of it."

How's that working out for you? He wouldn't ask that question out loud, but it riled him nonetheless.

"But you have a plan?" he prompted. Surely she was going to *do* something, not just pray about it.

"Not really. As I said, I'm not good at asking for money. And I don't have time to travel all over the countryside making presentations, even if I was good at that kind of thing. Which I'm not."

"What about a loan? Family? Friends?"

"No one around here is particularly well-to-do, and even if they were, I wouldn't dream of taking advantage of loved ones that way."

He'd never had loved ones, so he wouldn't know. He shrugged noncommittally and glanced away.

"I'll deal with it," she promised with a shaky laugh. "The cup is half full until it's not, right?"

"If you say so." He wasn't convinced.

"I do. And I need to concentrate on what I *can* do. Take care of my teenagers. If this is the last group I'll be able to help then I want to do all I can for them. The real work starts tomorrow. They'll learn all kinds of exciting skills useful in ranching. You're always welcome to join in. Anytime you want, okay?"

"Okay," he agreed, knowing even as he acknowledged her offer that he'd never take her up on it. Yes, he needed to learn everything he could about the ranching lifestyle, but he wasn't about to hang out with a bunch of juvenile delinquents, no matter how redeemable Alexis believed them to be.

Just one more fact in a long line of them that Alexis didn't need to know.

Griff shrugged on a new burgundy-colored Western shirt and snapped it up, then tucked the tails into his blue jeans. Country comfort beat suits and ties by a mile. These new clothes fit him and his new lifestyle—or what would be his life, once he was settled. Now all he needed was to buy a couple of horses and set himself up on a nice little patch of land.

Despite Alexis's offer, he had no intention of spending any time at Redemption Ranch observing her with the teenagers. He couldn't think of anything that would bring more discomfort to him. The sooner he scouted out his new land and made his purchase, the sooner he could walk away from this ranch—and Alexis—for good.

The sooner, the better, as far as he was concerned.

Staying here was messing with his head. He'd promised himself he wouldn't get involved in another person's problems ever again. He was dealing with enough issues of his own—a whole slew of nasty stuff that would take a lifetime to conquer. But then he'd butted his head in where it didn't belong with Devon, and had effectively broken his own promise to himself. As if that wasn't bad enough, ever since Alexis had opened up to him the night before, he couldn't seem to put her out of his mind.

Not his problem.

Except for the fact that he could help her.

As if that counted for anything.

He dabbed his fingers into his hair gel and jammed them through the thick, unruly tips of his hair. As usual, it was difficult to tame. Just as his emotions were right now. He couldn't stop thinking about Alexis. He *had* to stop thinking about her.

He hadn't had much experience dealing with ministry-type organizations, but how different could it really be? He was a venture capitalist. His skill set lent itself to finding people to support ideas. If anything, the fact that Alexis's program was a ministry ought to make it easier to fund. Religious folks loved to give to a good cause, right? It was all in how it was displayed.

Frankly, Griff couldn't understand why Alexis was having such a hard time handling that aspect of the program. With her upbeat personality and dynamic good looks, she ought to be raking in the moola with ease. Clearly, her presentation needed a bit of tweaking.

But not by him.

Not. By. Him.

He scowled at his reflection. When was he going to learn to mind his own business? Now would be a good time—before he found himself neck deep in Alexis's problems and headed for another broken heart.

No. Not for him, thanks.

Not today. Not ever.

He headed out of the bunkhouse, intending to hop in his sports car and scout the neighborhood on his own. If nothing else, getting the lay of the land would possibly help him hone in on what he was really looking for. At the moment his plans were still rather vague. Too much so.

He'd been in a hurry to get out of Houston after Caro had slam-dunked both his personal and professional lives. He wasn't usually the kind of man who went off half-cocked. He was a planner.

Just look at what had happened when he'd set his reservations aside and traveled by the seat of his pants. When he'd followed through on his whim to come to Serendipity, he'd ended up as the unexpected and, at least initially, unwelcomed guest of a woman who'd already bitten off far more than she could chew with this flailing ministry of hers. The last thing she needed was to have to deal with him underneath her feet. He was self-aware enough to realize he wasn't exactly the easiest fellow to get along with—the previous evening's dinner fiasco being a prime example. Surely, Alexis was wishing Griff would go elsewhere by now, no matter how graciously she treated him to his face.

Jingling his keys in his hand, he exited the bunkhouse and was almost to his little red coupe when he spotted Alexis in the yard. She and the teenagers were huddled in front of the house. From a distance, he couldn't see what they were looking at, but whatever it was, it was clearly holding their interest, and they certainly sounded animated. The excited muddle of voices and occasional exclamation easily reached his ears.

He pressed the button on the key fob that unlocked his car. It chirped in response, drawing Alexis's attention. She waved and he returned the gesture—he didn't want to appear rude, after all. He hadn't expected her to signal for him to join them, but her gesture was impossible to ignore.

He hesitated. He'd promised himself he'd simply avoid the teenagers and their drama. Problem solved. But then Alexis laughed and gestured again. Whatever stress had been weighing her down the night before seemed to have dissipated. He envied her the ability to put her problems aside so easily. The light in her eyes was contagious. He supposed it wouldn't hurt for him to say hello and have a quick look at what was going on up there at the front of the house.

As he approached, he caught a glimpse of what he hadn't been able to see from his car. Around the front of the house was a man in a sheriff's uniform, a woman casually dressed in jeans and a cotton pullover and a couple of large black dogs of different breeds.

What were the police doing here? Had he misread Alexis's expression? Had she been ushering him over because she was distressed? Had one of the kids gotten into some more serious trouble?

His gaze traveled over the group of teenagers until it settled on Devon, who was slouched against the porch railing, methodically scuffing his combat boots into the dirt at his feet. No one, not the cop or anyone else, appeared to be paying any particular attention to the boy, which for once was a good thing.

Griff released his breath. He didn't know why he'd immediately assumed it might be Devon who was in trouble. Perhaps it was because Griff had encountered one or two scuffles with the law when he was about Devon's age.

He was glad he was wrong, and a little annoyed with himself that it had been Devon who'd immediately popped into his mind with the possibility of trouble. He knew from experience that the other two boys were just as likely, if not more likely, to have initiated some kind of disturbance.

"What's all this?" he asked as he reached Alexis's

side. He lowered his voice so that the teens wouldn't hear him. "Not a problem going on here, I hope."

"What?" Her eyes widened, filled with confusion. Then she giggled. "Oh, you mean Eli. He's only wearing his uniform to put a little bit of the fear of God into the kids—lets them know right off the bat that I have friends in high places."

Griff quirked a grin. "Wise man."

"It doesn't hurt my cause," Alexis admitted with a knowing smile. She pointed to the woman at the sheriff's side. "His wife, Mary, is one of my best friends. She trains K9s for local police departments. Eli and his dog Bullet were her first trainees."

"Her husband was her first client? How does that work?"

"Well, he wasn't her husband at the time." Alexis laughed. "They fell in love during the process. Isn't that romantic?"

"Very," Griff agreed, suppressing his skepticism. Mary and Eli appeared happy, but for how long? Romance was nothing more than a ruse, a way for people to get what they wanted—which wasn't love. Not in the long term, anyway.

Griff wandered nearer to where Devon was standing and silently observed as Eli and Mary demonstrated some basic commands with their dogs. He had to admit the process was interesting to watch, a fascinating glimpse into K9 training. Eli hid a tennis ball and allowed Bullet to sniff it out, then cracked the teenagers up when he showed the face he'd drawn onto the orange ball with a felt-tipped pen.

"Aren't they just the cutest couple?" Alexis gushed, moving closer to Griff's side and pressing his forearm.

Griff suppressed the urge to gag, but thankfully Alexis didn't appear to notice Griff's aversion to the conversation. "And they're so sweet taking time out of their busy schedules to work with my kids. It's become sort of a tradition now that whenever a new batch of teenagers arrives, they come over and do a little demonstration with their dogs. You can see how the K9s hold everyone's interest."

Which was mostly true. The teens were surprisingly open with the dogs, if not the sheriff and his wife.

All except for one.

Devon.

The young man couldn't have appeared less interested in the scene in front of him. He didn't even look at the dogs, much less interact with them. He just stared at the ground as if he were willing a chasm to open and swallow him.

Griff could relate.

He laid a hand on Alexis's arm and nodded toward Devon. "Not all the kids," he whispered in a voice meant only for her ears. He led her a few feet away from where the boy was standing.

The smile dropped from Alexis's lips but quickly returned. "Give him a little more time to adjust to these new surroundings," she whispered back. "We'll get him where he needs to go. He'll be fine."

"Will he?" Griff's voice was low and coarse. For boys like Devon, there was no such thing as *fine*.

"Of course he will. Some kids just take a little longer to work things out than others do. He'll come around eventually." Her smile was sincere, and Griff realized she believed her own rhetoric. "Don't worry, Griff. I have my eye on Devon. I have every intention of showering him with the extra love and attention he clearly needs."

Was that how it worked? Why she was successful rehabilitating the teens?

Love and attention.

Two words so far out of Griff's realm of experience that it was next to impossible for him to even begin to comprehend what Alexis did here at Redemption Ranch.

"Trust me," she assured him.

He didn't dare. Not even with all of the kindness she'd showed to him and the teenagers in her care.

Run, Devon, he thought, his pulse escalating despite his best efforts to tamp it down. *Run, and don't look back.*

Chapter Five

Griff was certainly acting a little strange. Alexis cast a sideways glance at the man standing next to her. He had an odd, unreadable expression on his face and was shifting from foot to foot as if he was about to bolt.

She didn't understand the man. Whenever they conversed, she always felt as though there was an underlying current to what he was saying that she didn't get at all.

"Where were you headed in your car?" she asked Griff as Eli and Mary wound up their demonstration.

Griff jingled his keys in his palm. "Nowhere in particular. I thought I'd drive around town a little bit and try to start to get a decent lay of the land. Maybe see if I could connect with that real-estate agent you mentioned to me. Her name was Marge, right?"

"Right. Marge Thompson. Good idea. But before you go looking up Marge, you really ought to speak with Jo Spencer. She owns the Cup O' Jo Café. I'm sure you saw it when you entered town. Jo will most likely turn out to be a better connection for you in finding your new home than even our official real-estate agent."

"How so?"

"When it comes to Serendipity, Jo knows everything about everyone. Folks of all ages gather at the café. The gossip train begins and ends with Jo, and she's the prime conductor. If anyone is selling their property, or even just mulling it over, Jo will know about it. All you have to do is tell her what you're looking for and she'll advise you of your best options right on the spot. Not only that, but she'll help you in ways you can't even imagine. You'll probably get a more accurate reading of what you're looking for from Jo than you even realize you need right now."

He raised an eyebrow. "Sounds promising. So then I just stop by the café and ask for Jo?"

Alexis chuckled. "Oh, you won't have to ask for her. She'll find you first. Trust me on this one. I would venture to guess that she already knows you're staying here at the ranch, and possibly already the specifics on the plans for your future."

"I'm not so sure I like the sound of that," he admitted, shifting from foot to foot.

Alexis noticed his skittish behavior but waved off his concern. She guessed he was probably just nervous about being discussed by everyone in town. He'd soon realize that every neighbor in Serendipity was simply a friend he hadn't met yet. "Jo has the largest heart in the county. She'll be a really good ally for you."

"Humph," he grunted. "Anything else I should know before I take off?"

"You know what? If you can wait around for a few more minutes, I'll go along with you and introduce you to Jo personally. I have a couple of errands I need to run, anyway. We can kill two birds with one stone, so to speak."

Griff hesitated and shifted his gaze away from hers. She could see him debating the issue in his mind.

"I don't know…" he hedged.

"About what? Killing birds?" she joked, hoping to lighten him up a bit.

He didn't so much as crack a grin. Tough sell, that one.

"Look. You don't have to wait for me if you don't want to. I'll understand if you feel you've got too much to do to hang around here any longer. I'm sure you're anxious to get settled in your new life."

"I'll wait." With such a clipped answer, made with such tight body language, she wondered what kind of company he was going to be. But she'd promised Vivian that she'd be helpful and *nice,* and besides, she really did have things to do in town.

Eli and Mary approached and Alexis did her best to put her troublesome thoughts about Griff aside.

"Thank you guys again for coming out," she told her friends. "It always sets the kids up for their month of new learning experiences."

"Of course. Where else would we be other than here with you and the teenagers? And if that wasn't enough of a reason, I've got another. Watching Eli perform with Bullet stirs up whole realms of good memories for me." Mary kissed her palm and blew it at Eli, who grinned and made a grand gesture of snatching her invisible token of affection from the air and planting it on his cheek.

"You two are almost nauseating in your happiness."

"Aren't we, though?" Mary agreed with a blissful sigh. She linked arms with Alexis and drew her forward, away from the two men, and then leaned in with a conspiratorial wink. "Now who is the tall drink of water you were just speaking with? A new employee?"

"Oh, goodness, no," Alexis exclaimed. "Griff is in no way affiliated with the ranch, except as a guest. He's a friend of Viv's from Houston."

"I didn't realize Vivian was in town."

"She isn't."

Mary chuckled. "This guy Griff came out here on his own?"

"Hmm," Alexis answered vaguely. "It's a long story, and I'm sure an amusing one, now that I'm a little distanced from it. Not so hilarious when it actually happened, but you know how it is with life stories. Let's walk toward the stable and I'll fill you in on the juicy details."

Eli and Griff were deep in conversation, as well, and they followed at a distance behind Alexis and Mary. Farther behind them were the kids, escorted by the counselors. Keeping her voice low so she wouldn't be overheard, Alexis divulged the tale of finding a strange, handsome man making breakfast in her kitchen.

"How romantic," Mary said as Alexis wound her story down.

"Trust me, it was the absolutely furthest thing from romantic that there could possibly be. He nearly frightened the daylights out of me. I was on the verge of calling the police on him. I wonder how it would have turned out if I had."

"Yes, but still—a handsome stranger suddenly arrives in your life. Sounds like the beginning of a love story to me. It kind of reminds me of when Will showed up unexpectedly at Samantha's store. And we both know how that turned out."

Alexis's skin prickled. She had to admit, privately, at least, that there were many nuances of the situation that mirrored what had happened between their other best friend, Samantha, when she first met her husband Will back when he and his little daughter were newly arrived in town. But there was no conceivable way the outcome would be the same.

"You're beginning to sound a lot like Vivian," she accused lightheartedly, not wanting to admit to the truth of what Mary had said.

"Don't tell me Vivian is playing matchmaker."

Heat rose to Alexis's face. She hoped Mary couldn't see her distress.

"She *is*," Mary exclaimed. "How exciting."

"How *annoying* is more like it. Vivian and her crazy schemes. She manipulated a situation that was rather touchy to begin with and now poor Griff is paying the price for her foolishness."

"Well, not really, honey. It seems to me that he got a pretty good deal out of it, getting to stay at Redemption Ranch. With you," Mary added impishly.

"I'm sure Griff doesn't see it that way, especially since I relegated him to the bunkhouse."

"You didn't."

"Yes, I did, and I'm proud of it. It wasn't as if I could allow him to stay at the house with me. Can you imagine what people would say?"

"Oh, I imagine people are going to come to whatever conclusions they please anyway, no matter where you've got Griff bunking. But I still say meeting you was a good thing for him. At least he knows someone in town who can help him find what he's looking for."

"I suppose. Speaking of which, I need to get the kids started with the horses. I promised Griff I'd take him into town and introduce him to Jo Spencer. Just to get the ball rolling, so to speak."

Mary clapped a hand over her mouth but was unable to stifle a laugh. "That ought to stir things up."

Alexis's throat constricted and she coughed to loosen her breath. She hadn't thought through the implications of how it would look to the townsfolk when she went around personally introducing Griff to everyone. If Mary was seeing romantic possibilities between Alexis and Griff, then Jo was bound to imagine the most fantastical scenario imaginable, what with her flair for the dramatic.

Alexis didn't especially look forward to the flak they were going to receive, but she supposed she could handle it. She was used to the inner workings of small-town life. But poor Griff, fresh off of a broken heart, might not be so acquiescent. The last thing she'd want for him would be to discover he'd been romantically paired with her by ladies with vivid imaginations and too much time on their hands.

"Oh, no. I already promised him," she said with a groan.

"Don't worry about it, sweetie. Griff's presence in town will be discovered sooner or later, if it hasn't been already. This way you can take the offense in letting people know why he's here instead of letting rumors percolate before they come to you."

On the defense, more like. But Mary was right. Better to have the opportunity to offer as many facts right up front at the beginning to waylay the inevitable speculation.

She reached the stable and stepped through the large double doors, inhaling deeply. One of her favorite scents was the barn with its horses and hay. If she could, she'd live on horseback 24/7.

"All right, ladies and gentlemen," she announced. "It's high time you guys started contributing some effort into the ranch. Who wants to muck out some stalls?"

Her question was met with a collective groan.

"It's not all bad," she promised. "You'll also get to spend some time with the horse that you'll be caring for throughout the month. Anyone here know how to ride?"

Only one girl, Destiny, raised her hand, and she snatched it back down again when she realized she was the only one who knew anything about horses.

"No matter. We have expert wranglers on staff to teach you everything you'll need to know. Fun, fun!"

She chuckled under her breath at the mixed reactions. The kids were acting as though they weren't interested, yet their eyes were alight with curiosity. They didn't know they were about to meet their equine therapists. Alexis had found that animals oftentimes met the teenagers' needs better even than humans could do.

"Go ahead and take a walk through the stable. The names of the horses are on the stall doors. Pick out whichever mount looks good to you and spend some time getting to know your horse. There's a bucket of carrots hanging from that beam over there," she continued, gesturing toward the bucket. "You're welcome to feed your new horse a snack."

The teenagers burst into chatter as they rushed to pick out their horses.

Only Devon held back. Alexis knew enough of his past to take an educated guess as to why he wasn't responding as well as the others. His mother had passed away a couple of years ago after being diagnosed with stage-four lung cancer. His father was an affluent politician who was often out of town, leaving Alexis to wonder just how much time he spent with his son. Relationship building was bound to be tough for a kid like that.

Caring for a horse might be especially beneficial to Devon, allowing him to connect with a live creature who would respond to his attention. And it would give him something worthwhile to do with his time, a trait she'd discovered was often lacking in the teens' lives.

The other kids had all selected their horses and were being attended to by the wranglers, who were showing them how to feed and groom their mounts. Alexis started to move in Devon's direction but came up short as Griff appeared at the boy's side.

"You like horses?" Griff asked, laying a hand on the boy's shoulder.

Devon shrugged noncommittally.

"Sure." Griff didn't appear ruffled by the teen's moodiness. "I get it. You've probably never been up close and personal with one. Am I right?"

Again, Devon shrugged, but he looked up and met Griff's gaze.

"You're gonna like this. Here, let's go pick you out a decent mount." He pressed the young man's shoulder, urging him toward the stalls.

Alexis watched inquisitively as Griff led Devon

down the row of stalls, reading the names on the doors as they went. "Midnight. Beauty. Shazam."

Griff turned and grinned at Alexis. "Wow, lady, you've picked such original names for your horses," he teased.

"Lady is the next stall down," Alexis quipped. "Try the appaloosa across the way. His name is Pitonio. Original enough for you?"

"I've never heard of the name before," he agreed with a chuckle. "Here, Devon. Let's give him a carrot and see how he responds to you."

Devon backed up and shoved his hands into the pockets of his trench coat, fear flashing in his brown eyes as he stared at the spotted horse. Alexis nearly stepped in to slow Griff down, but something held her back.

"When I was about your age," Griff said in a storytelling tone of voice, "I had trouble at home. I didn't like to be around any more often than I absolutely had to be. You get what I'm saying?"

Devon's gaze darkened and his body language remained muted. "Yeah."

"Well, there was this ranch I passed every day on the way to my high school." He reached across the top of the stall door and ran his hand along Pitonio's withers. "There were these two wild mustangs in one pasture. I'm pretty certain no one ever rode on either of them." He gestured for Devon to move closer. To Alexis's surprise, the boy complied.

Griff held out his hand palm up and placed a carrot across it, allowing Pitonio to nibble on it. Then he offered a carrot for Devon to feed the horse, all the while distracting the boy by continuing the story.

"I used to crawl through the fence and spend hours with those two horses. They were my best buddies back then. Horses have a sense about people, you see. They didn't judge me by my hair or the clothes I wore. Here. Just hold your hand flat, son. Pitonio won't bite."

"Did you ever ride one of them?" Devon asked.

Alexis leaned in to hear the answer.

"I believe I'm the only one who ever did. I earned their trust little by little. I used to save my apples from lunch to share with them."

"Cool," Devon replied, although Alexis wasn't certain if that was in response to what Griff had said or because Pitonio nibbled the carrot right off Devon's hand.

"Give the horse a chance, okay, buddy?"

Devon nodded and hesitantly ran a hand down Pitonio's muzzle.

Griff's gaze met Alexis's and her heart did a little flip. When he smiled at her she swept in a breath that made her feel dizzy.

He'd accomplished more in ten minutes than she might have been able to do in the whole month. He'd set Devon down a positive path. He'd reached out and showed the boy it was okay to connect. He'd thrown the young man a lifeline.

Did he realize how amazing he was? Because right then and there, Alexis did.

Griff gawked as he and Alexis entered Cup O' Jo's Café. The outside of the building had looked like something out of an old Western movie, from the clapboard siding to the hitching post and water trough out in front of the wooden sidewalk. Inside was a different ambience altogether. He was surprised at the modern coffee shop feel the place exuded, complete with computers lining the tables along the back wall.

With it being the middle of the afternoon, he hadn't expected the café to have many customers, but at least half the booths were filled with everyone from a chattering group of preteens to three old men wearing matching bib overalls. Alexis had been right when she'd told him that folks of all ages gathered here.

When the patrons spotted Griff, their conversations came to a momentary halt before the buzz started again—he suspected most of it having to do with him. The hair prickled on the back of his neck as he acknowledged openly curious stares and friendly waves. The townspeople looked harmless enough, but Griff felt as if he was about to be eaten alive by a pack of hungry lions.

This was a bad, bad idea.

Alexis apparently recognized his hesitation because she grabbed his hand and tugged him forward.

"Hey, Jo," she called to the curly redheaded woman behind the cash register.

Jo looked up from the stack of receipts she was ordering and squealed in delight. Her ample frame bounced with every movement and her lime-green T-shirt proclaimed Ready or Not, Here I Come.

An apt saying, Griff thought wryly.

"It's about time you brought your young man around," Jo exclaimed, prancing out from behind the counter and enveloping first Alexis and then Griff in her vigorous embrace.

Griff stiffened. He wasn't big on public displays of affection, most especially directed at him by a woman he'd just met. And she was wrong on two counts—he wasn't young and he wasn't Alexis's man.

"You must be Griff," Jo said, her voice boisterous and loud. Griff was thankful when she took a step back, leaving him at least a modicum of personal space.

Griff still felt as if he had lead running through his veins, but for Alexis's sake if nothing else, he forced himself to smile. "And I would have to say you are Jo Spencer. Nice to meet you."

"Yep, that's me, dear. The infamous Jo Spencer. I'm not a bit surprised you've heard of me."

Maybe not, but Griff was definitely surprised that *she'd* heard of *him*.

"We're here for the latest 4-1-1," Alexis informed Jo, "but I also wanted to introduce Griff to the best cheeseburger in Texas."

"You've got it. Let me get you kids settled in a booth so you can relax while you wait. Right this way, my dears."

Griff smothered a chuckle as he followed the dynamic hostess to their table. He hadn't been referred to as a kid in—well, it had been a long time. Jo seated them but didn't offer a menu.

"Two cheeseburgers," Jo said. "And I know Alexis wants a diet cola. What would you care to drink, Griff?"

"Water is fine, thank you."

"Be sure to save some room for dessert," Jo warned as she left the table to turn in their order and tend to her other customers.

"She's quite serious about saving room for dessert," Alexis informed him. "Our Phoebe Hawkins bakes the best pastries on the planet. Cookies and pies, too. You'll have a hard time choosing."

"Jo seems to know you pretty well," he commented after Jo had dropped off their drinks.

"Oh, she knows everyone in town. Diet cola has been my standing order since I used to come here with the Little Chicks as a teenager."

"Little Chicks?"

Alexis giggled. "That's what the boys on the football team nicknamed my two best friends and me when we were teenagers—probably because of our chatter. You know how high school girls are. We grew up, of course, but the nickname stuck. I don't know whether it's a blessing or a curse, but most folks around here still see us that way."

"Who are the other lucky ladies?"

"You've met Mary, and my other BFF is Samantha, the owner of Sam's Grocery."

Griff was more fascinated by the glimpse into Alexis's world than he should have been, gathering hints as to what made her the extraordinary woman she was. At the moment she was so cheerful she was glowing and gushing. She took his breath away.

Her expression now was a far cry from the way he'd found her crying over her bills in her office. Had she discovered a solution to her dilemma since then?

"How goes the fund-raising?"

Instantly the smile dropped from her lips and her blue eyes took on a translucent quality. "It's not."

Way to go, Haddon.

He'd just singlehandedly managed to ball up her happiness and heartlessly sling it into the trash.

A strained silence reigned between them as Jo arrived with their burgers, set them on the table and returned to the counter.

Griff bit into his, chewed and swallowed but tasted nothing. The problem wasn't the cheeseburger. It was him.

Alexis opened the ketchup bottle and turned it over, popping the bottom with the flat of her palm to start the flow. Nothing happened for a moment and then suddenly it all came out in a rush, globbing onto her plate.

Alexis laughed, joy instantly returning to her countenance. The tension dissipated, but the lump in Griff's throat grew.

"Count on me to make a mess. If there's a way to do it, I will find it. I don't suppose you need some ketchup with your fries?"

Griff spooned some of her ketchup onto his plate.

"Problem solved," he said with a grin, relieved that the friction between them had passed and that he hadn't completely ruined her day.

"Can we just not talk about my financial concerns right now?" she asked in a husky voice, her smile wavering. "We're here to try to settle your affairs. Right?"

"Of course," he agreed, though privately he wondered how she could set aside her own issues so easily. It was as if she was able to compartmentalize her life and had simply chosen to stuff the bad segments somewhere in the back of her mind.

The part that concerned him was the certainty that her problems weren't going to dissolve simply by ignoring them. Eventually she'd have to deal with her issues. Still, he supposed she knew that and he envied her ability to see the bright side of life, especially since he was the worst kind of pessimist.

The conversation turned inconsequential. Alexis kept up a stream of the mundane and Griff was relieved to follow her lead.

As promised, Jo returned with dessert. Griff was saved from having to make the choice himself because Jo, in a warmly imperious way, had decided for him. He certainly couldn't complain about her choice: a mouthwatering peach cobbler with crumbles of brown sugar on top. She served Alexis and Griff and then brought a square for herself and pulled up a chair to join them at their table.

Griff took a bite of the cobbler and groaned in ecstasy. "I've got to agree completely about Phoebe's baking skills. This is the best cobbler I've ever had the pleasure of tasting. Please give her my compliments."

"Oh, there's no doubt about Phoebe's talent, my dear, and I'll be sure to tell her you enjoyed her handiwork," Jo agreed with a boisterous nod of her head that sent her red curls bobbing. "Phoebe was a well-known chef in New York City before she made her home in Serendipity. Now she just blesses us here in town with her God-given talent."

Griff let the "God-given" part slide, since it appeared folks around here just talked that way, but he did wonder why a successful big-city chef would make her home in Serendipity.

"She met my nephew Chance—the fellow who made that scrumptious cheeseburger you just chowed down. Then she fell in love, and that's how it happened."

Jo was practically reading his mind. It was a little disconcerting for her to be so completely spot-on with her observations. Alexis hadn't been kidding when she'd said Jo had an uncanny ability to read people.

"Enough about my family," Jo continued, slapping her palms flat against the tabletop. "Let's get to the good stuff. I understand you're looking to settle down in this great town of ours. Good choice, by the way. We're happy to have you."

"Thank you," Griff responded automatically, although he really wasn't interested in whether or not the townsfolk cared about what he did. He did like Jo, though. Who wouldn't?

"He's looking to buy a spread of land. For horses, right, Griff?" Alexis asked.

"Large? Medium? Small?" Jo queried right on Alexis's heels.

"I, uh, don't really know for sure," he reluctantly admitted. He didn't want these women to think he was impetuous, leaping before he looked. But wasn't that exactly what he'd done? Just as Alexis consciously ignored her problems, Griff had ditched his sensible life in Houston to chase after a vague pipedream.

"Yes on the horses," he said after a moment's thought. "A small herd, just for my own benefit. So I'm probably not looking at needing too big of a spread."

"You don't plan on making a living off the land?" Jo asked.

Griff's gaze met Alexis's. She smiled and nodded her encouragement.

"I don't… That is…" he stammered. How was he going to explain that he didn't really need or want a working ranch, and that he was set financially and didn't need to be making a yearly income? His investments provided more than enough for what he needed to live.

If he blurted out that kind of information, and if peo-

We'd like to send you two free books from the series you are enjoying now. Your two books have a combined cover price of over $10, but are yours to keep absolutely FREE! We'll even send you two wonderful surprise gifts. You can't lose!

Each of your FREE books is filled with joy, faith and traditional values as men and women open their hearts to each other and join together on a spiritual journey.

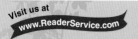

GET 2 FREE BOOKS!

HURRY!
Return this card today to get 2 FREE Books and 2 FREE Bonus Gifts!

YES! Please send me the **2 FREE books** and **2 FREE gifts** for which I qualify. I understand that I am under no obligation to purchase anything further, as explained on the back of this card.

PLACE FREE GIFTS SEAL HERE

❏ I prefer the regular-print edition
105/305 IDL GEJZ

❏ I prefer the larger-print edition
122/322 IDL GEJZ

FIRST NAME

LAST NAME

ADDRESS

APT.#

CITY

STATE/PROV.

ZIP/POSTAL CODE

⬧ HARLEQUIN™ READER SERVICE—Here's How It Works:

Accepting your 2 free Love Inspired® Romance books and 2 free gifts (gifts valued at approximately $10.00) places you under no obligation to buy anything. You may keep the books and gifts and return the shipping statement marked "cancel." If you do not cancel, about a month later we'll send you 6 additional books and bill you just $4.74 each for the regular-print edition or $5.24 each for the larger-print edition in the U.S. or $5.24 each for the regular-print edition or $5.74 each for the larger-print edition in Canada. That is a savings of at least 21% off the cover price. It's quite a bargain! Shipping and handling is just 50¢ per book in the U.S. and 75¢ per book in Canada.* You may cancel at any time, but if you choose to continue, every month we'll send you 6 more books, which you may either purchase at the discount price or return to us and cancel your subscription. *Terms and prices subject to change without notice. Prices do not include applicable taxes. Sales tax applicable in N.Y. Canadian residents will be charged applicable taxes. Offer not valid in Quebec. Books received may not be as shown. All orders subject to credit approval. Credit or debit balances in a customer's account(s) may be offset by any other outstanding balance owed by or to the customer. Please allow 4 to 6 weeks for delivery. Offer available while quantities last.

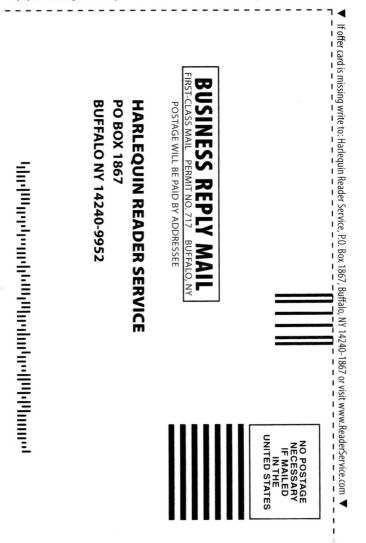

▲ If offer card is missing write to: Harlequin Reader Service, P.O. Box 1867, Buffalo, NY 14240-1867 or visit www.ReaderService.com ▲

BUSINESS REPLY MAIL
FIRST-CLASS MAIL   PERMIT NO. 717   BUFFALO, NY

POSTAGE WILL BE PAID BY ADDRESSEE

HARLEQUIN READER SERVICE
PO BOX 1867
BUFFALO NY 14240-9952

NO POSTAGE
NECESSARY
IF MAILED
IN THE
UNITED STATES

ple became aware of his affluence, they would change. He was willing to venture that even Alexis would become a different person around him if she knew the whole truth.

"Let's just start you off by finding you some horses and a small spread of land," Jo said, taking the heat off of Griff, almost as if she sensed his distress. "The rest of it is just details, right?" She waved her arm dismissively.

"We were hoping maybe you had a few leads for us," Alexis said. "We'll be stopping by Marge's, of course, but we thought we'd ask you first."

"I'm glad you did, dear. Now, I haven't heard of anything as of yet, but I'll keep my ears open and start spreading the word that Griff is looking for land."

Griff groaned inwardly. This conversation was going downhill fast. He didn't want the whole town up in his business. He supposed he'd pictured simply investigating on his own and arranging a quiet deal.

"I'm not sure if—" he started, but Alexis interrupted him.

"Tell everyone they can contact me directly and I'll pass on the information to Griff, since he's staying at Redemption Ranch—in the bunkhouse, with the wranglers."

Griff wanted to bang his head against a wall. By mistake he'd involved a couple of females with his challenge and in a matter of seconds they'd managed to completely take it out of his hands.

Could this get any worse?

Chapter Six

Alexis sneezed repeatedly as she opened the rickety wooden door to the little-used shed where she stored her seasonal decorations. Samantha and Will had promised to come over and help her organize the mess, but they'd been busy remodeling Sam's Grocery and Alexis hadn't wanted to push the issue. It was just a bunch of old boxes. And most of the time they were out of sight, out of mind.

Except now, when she needed something.

She had grand dreams of color-coded plastic bins neatly spaced and carefully labeled and stored on shelving units. She'd be able to walk in and select the correct bins within seconds. No muss, no fuss. Her current mode of organization, such as it was, consisted of a bunch of old apple boxes labeled with hand-drawn scribbles in colored markers. The whole lot was haphazardly tossed into unsorted piles.

It would take her half a day just to plow through the clutter and find the items she was searching for.

Vivian was due this weekend. She didn't usually visit in the middle of a Mission Month, but this was a special occasion—at least to Vivian, who always snapped up a reason to celebrate.

Alexis usually completely agreed with her twin in this. She was a people person who loved community events and gatherings to rejoice with others over milestones. However, the milestone in question this time was their birthday, and Vivian expected a party. A *large* celebration, filled to the brim with merry friends and neighbors.

Alexis would just as soon have ignored this particular occasion. After all, once a woman hit a certain age, birthdays took on an entirely different significance. She would rather forget she was growing older, especially this year, when everything she had to show for what she'd accomplished in her life was threatening to crash and burn around her.

But for Vivian's sake, Alexis would put aside her own reticence and go to whatever effort was necessary to make their birthday a special celebration. Despite their differences and whatever difficulties they may have had with each other over the years, her twin was the dearest person in the world to her. To see Vivian's face glowing with joy and delight was worth whatever discomfort Alexis might glean from the occasion.

She pulled at the boxes stacked in front, reading the labels aloud. "Christmas. Christmas. Easter. Winter."

Now where were the boxes marked Birthday? Alexis groaned. "Probably stuck in a back corner somewhere, lodged under a dozen other boxes."

The front boxes kind-of, sort-of formed a ladder. Maybe if she gingerly stepped up a few notches she would be able to see—

"Do you always mutter to yourself?" Griff's amused voice came from behind her, sending her reeling.

Literally.

Her arms wind-milled as she sought to keep her balance. She reached for something to steady herself and caught nothing but air. Then large hands encompassed her waist as Griff gently lifted her to the ground. He continued to hold her while she found her feet, his breath warm at the nape of her neck.

The air left her lungs in a whoosh as if her whole body had made contact with the earth. Her sight tunneled as dizziness threatened to overwhelm her. She suspected her reaction had little to do with her near fall and significantly more to do with the man who still had his arms around her waist.

She forced herself to breathe. What a silly goose she was being. Vivian was right. She'd been too long without a date if the mere presence of a man could send her reeling like a teenager with her first crush.

No, attraction couldn't possibly be what she was feeling. It was the catastrophe of a near disaster that had her pulse threading rapidly, not the fact that Griff had *still* not stepped away from her.

"You don't ever talk to yourself?" she challenged, turning in his arms. Her heart galloped when her gaze met his, for she knew in that instant that he was just as affected by her nearness as she was by his. His gray-blue eyes were glowing.

Which was wrong in more ways than she could count, starting with the fact that he was a guest on her ranch. And he was a close friend of Vivian's. And he wasn't a died-in-the-wool rancher. And—

Eep!

"You don't sing with the radio in your car?" she suggested.

"I wouldn't subject anyone in this world to my complete inability to carry a tune, least of all me."

"Well, I do. Like the sound of my own voice, that is—whether singing or talking." A woman needed the ability to laugh at herself, and that was exactly what Alexis did. "I find if I speak aloud I come to conclusions I might not otherwise have drawn."

Griff gestured toward the boxes. "And what conclusions have you reached today with your self-chatter?"

Alexis grinned up at him and sighed dramatically. "That the boxes I'm looking for are probably hiding in the shadows somewhere out of sight. At the very bottom of the pile, no doubt."

"No doubt," he agreed with a dry chuckle.

She realized only afterward that her actions might be interpreted as being flirtatious. If she read the gleam in Griff's eyes correctly, he thought so, too. *Oh, boy.*

He saved her from the humiliation of frantically grasping for a safe avenue of conversation by asking, "What can I do to help you?"

"That's kind of you to offer, but I've got this under control." *Back away from the danger. Back slowly away.*

"I'm sure you do," Griff drawled, one side of his mouth crooking up at the corner. He leaned his elbow on one of the stacks of boxes. "But as the old saying goes, two heads are better than one. Or in this case, the strength of two pairs of shoulders. I'd hate to see you have to move all these boxes on your own when I'm standing right here with the muscle to help you."

He flexed for her, and even though she really, *really*

didn't want him to notice, she couldn't help the way her appreciative gaze followed the path of his biceps.

His grin widened. Yep. He'd noticed that she'd noticed.

"Why don't you tell me what exactly you're looking for and I'll move the boxes," he persisted.

"Oh, all right, then. It appears all my Christmas stuff is stored in front, and I'm looking for the boxes marked Birthday."

"Whose birthday?" he asked, going right to work.

She sighed again, for real this time. "Mine and Viv's. She's coming up this weekend to celebrate."

"Why didn't you say something? Happy birthday," he exclaimed, pausing for a moment before slinging another box aside.

"Why would I bring it up?" Alexis parried. "Believe me, it's something I'd rather forget. There comes a time in a woman's life when birthdays are better skimmed over than celebrated—and don't you dare ask me how old that is."

Griff swallowed a chuckle. "I don't have a death wish, thank you."

"Wise man. Your mama taught you well."

His lips twisted. "My mother didn't teach me much of anything, except to stay out of her way."

Alexis met his gaze and the pain registered in their gray-blue depths hit her like a strike to the gut. For maybe the first time since she'd known him, he was being completely honest with her, and she didn't know how to react.

"I'm sorry," she said softly, laying her hand on his shoulder.

He scoffed and forced a crooked grin. "It's nothing."

It wasn't "nothing," but she couldn't force the issue. After what she'd glimpsed in Griff's eyes, she felt even less like celebrating now than she had before.

"I'll bet Viv enjoys a party, huh?"

Not knowing how to offer him comfort, she allowed him to change the subject. "She does. So do I, as a matter of fact. I didn't say I don't enjoy celebrating special events. I love a good party as much as anyone. Just not so much when it comes to my birthday."

"That's dumb."

"Well, thank you," she responded dryly.

"No, I don't mean to imply that *you're* dumb," he said, grunting as he attempted to lift a particularly unwieldy box. "I get it. Your birthday gives you cause to reflect on life, and sometimes that's a painful thing. I expect all of us feel we could have done better in one way or another."

"Mmm," she agreed, her heart aching.

"But I'll bet there are a lot of folks who've been blessed by you and Viv over the years. You're both special women. That's something to celebrate."

"Nice save," she teased, ticking her index finger in the air, but internally she was grateful for the way he'd turned it around.

He shot a grin over his shoulder. "Thank you. I try."

Their gazes met and her breath lodged uncomfortably in her throat. The shed suddenly felt way too small for the two of them.

He disappeared behind a pile of boxes and then exclaimed in triumph. "I found it. The birthday box."

Alexis laughed. "Nice try. I hate to break it to you, but there's more than one. Three, to be exact. Keep looking. I'm sure they're close together. Or at least, I hope they are. I apologize for my lack of a system."

"What are you going to do with three boxes of birthday decorations?"

"Host a party, of course."

"Well, yeah, I figured, but I had no idea…" His voice turned low and husky and then his sentence dropped off completely.

"Griff? Are you okay?"

"Yeah. Sure. Why wouldn't I be?" came his curt reply.

But he wasn't. No matter how off-hand he tried to sound about it, something was wrong.

"We may be a small town, but we do birthdays big around here." She wanted to offer her sympathy, vague as that might be, but how, when she didn't know what, exactly, was wrong? "Do you just have a small family affair where you're from?"

She realized as soon as she asked the question that she didn't even *know* where he was from. He'd shared precious little information about himself in the two weeks he'd been in Serendipity, and most of what she knew about him either came secondhand from Vivian or from what she'd overheard him share with Devon.

"I don't do birthdays," he admitted in a monotone. "Never have."

Alexis opened her mouth to ask him why not but then closed it again without speaking, realizing it wasn't some silly *women-of-a-certain-age* explanation with Griff. He made it sound as if he'd *never* celebrated a birthday, and then there was that comment about his mother. She suddenly felt very, very sad.

She hoped he'd offer more of his own volition, but

when he did not, she felt compelled to shift the focus away from him, as he had done for her.

"The other two birthday boxes have got to be back there somewhere. I hope."

"Yeah, I found them." Griff sounded relieved, and Alexis knew it wasn't because he'd been successful in locating the boxes, but because of the shift in conversation. "Let me maneuver them out for you."

"The party is Saturday night," she said, taking one of the boxes from him. "You are absolutely invited to be our guest."

He hesitated and shifted the remaining box he was holding to one arm.

"I don't know. I'm not much of a party kind of guy."

This was why Alexis suddenly felt it imperative that she get him to come to this one. Though she hadn't a clue what or who had so injured him in the past aside from his mother and the ex-girlfriend Vivian had mentioned, she wanted him to see a glimpse of his future here in Serendipity—a future full of life, and hope, and friends and neighbors who really cared about him. Maybe eventually he might find it in his heart to celebrate a birthday of his own, but in the meantime, she was determined to share her joy with him.

"I could really use your help." Maybe it wasn't fair, but Griff had already stepped up several times when she'd needed assistance, including today. Hopefully she could goad him into accepting her invitation if he thought he was needed.

He *was* needed. She just had to prove it to him.

"How so?" Was there interest gleaming from his eyes?

"I've enlisted the kids to help Vivian and me decorate the house. It could either be a blessing or a total disaster."

He chuckled dryly. "You want my opinion?"

"I want your *help*. I've seen how good you are with the teenagers."

"Me?" He sounded genuinely surprised.

"Yes, you."

"I don't even like kids."

She tilted her chin up at him and narrowed her gaze. "Is that right? Now, why don't I believe you?"

He shrugged and shifted his gaze to the stack of boxes. "Believe what you want."

"But you'll be there." She'd purposefully phrased her sentence as a statement and not a question. "At the house. Around three in the afternoon? I figure it will take us a couple of hours to get everything prepared and decorated, and folks will start arriving about five."

"A couple of *hours?* To decorate a house? How many people are you inviting to this party, again?"

It was her turn to shrug. "I'm never certain. Could be around a hundred, give or take a few."

"A hundred people. In your house."

"Yes, well, probably not all at once. And we're barbequing out front, so people don't all have to cram inside. Folks come and go as it suits them. Stop by for a few minutes to offer us their well-wishes. You know."

He shook his head and his eyes glazed over.

No, he clearly did not know of the many wonderful aspects of small-town life. But if Alexis had anything to say about it, he was about to learn.

Friday evening found Griff up to his elbows in papier-mâché. His head was spinning, still trying to

wrap his brain around what was happening to him. How had the Grainger women roped him into this whole party thing?

He had no idea. And yet here he was. He must be out of his mind. It sounded as if half the blooming town was going to show up. He could see his dreams of living a peaceful, anonymous life here in Serendipity swirling like wisps of smoke off into the horizon with no hope of him ever being able to catch them.

And instead of running after them—or just plain running for the hills—he was sitting at Alexis's dining table dunking roughly torn rectangular pieces of newspaper into some kind of goop made of flour and water and then plastering the whole sticky mess on the side of a red balloon.

"Tell me why we are doing this again?" he asked Vivian, who was seated at the opposite side of the table with her own balloon. When Alexis and Vivian had showed up on the bunkhouse doorstep earlier that evening, begging for him to help with party preparations, he'd balked and protested that he had too much to do. But there'd been two of them against one of him and they'd seen right through him and his pretense.

Alexis or Vivian on their own were formidable. Together, they were unstoppable, impossible to refuse. Which was the one and *only* reason he was sitting here right now with his hands covered in paste.

"We're making piñatas," Vivian explained with a long-suffering sigh, since she'd already walked him through the creation process when they'd first started. "Once this part is dry, we will paint them pretty colors. Then tomorrow we'll pop the balloon with a pin and fill the inside with goodies."

"That's all well and good—for kids. But isn't this an adult party?" He glanced at Viv, who for some reason had, upon her arrival, changed her outfit to match Alexis's light green, button-up shirt and black skinny jeans. She'd even pulled her hair back into a ponytail. It was the first time he'd ever seen Viv wear her hair that way. He couldn't fathom what she was trying to accomplish. If she meant to confuse him, she was wasting her time.

He could tell the difference between the twins in the blink of an eye. Alexis's eyes were a little brighter blue and her smile was softer. Prettier. And when she smiled, she had the hint of a dimple on her left cheek. He was grateful for how often he'd had a glimpse of that particular feature. Alexis was nearly always smiling.

"There will be kids there," Viv informed him, sounding a bit defensive. "Tons of them. Including Alexis's brood. It's a family occasion. But only one of the piñatas will be for the under-eighteen set. Why should the children have all the fun?"

Alexis appeared at the entranceway to the kitchen. "If Vivian had her way, we'd all be playing Pin the Tail on the Donkey."

"And what, I ask you, is wrong with that?" Vivian demanded playfully. "Nothing breaks the ice like a rousing game of Pin the Tail on the Donkey."

Griff met Alexis's gaze and she rolled her eyes. When she threw back her head and laughed, a chuckle rumbled from Griff's throat and warmth filled his chest. One thing he could say about Alexis was that being around her was never boring. She lived life as one adventure after another. If she ignored the bumps in the road, who could blame her? And who could resist helping her along the way?

Sparks of ideas went off in his mind like fireworks and a singular revelation hit him like a freight train. He was going to help her solve her financial problems with Redemption Ranch. He didn't know the exact moment he'd capitulated from his earlier vow not to get involved, but the resolution was suddenly crystal clear in his mind and had somehow, without his knowledge, lodged deep in his heart.

It was the right thing to do, to assist a woman who dedicated her life to doing things for others. Even this party was for her sister's sake, not her own.

He could help her. And he would.

"Who wants cookies?" Alexis tempted, producing a platter of fresh-from-the-oven oatmeal-raisin cookies. "I can't have my worker bees going hungry."

Griff had only ever had store-bought cookies, he realized as he wiped his hand on a towel so he could indulge in the treat. The sight, smell and touch of a warm cookie was a fresh, invigoratingly new experience for him, and that was nothing to say of the first scrumptious bite. It defied words.

A bell pealed from within the kitchen.

"Oh, that's the cake. No peeking while it's cooling, Vivian. I want it to be a surprise for you. I have to slip out and speak to the counselors about the kids' progress. I'll be back in a minute."

"She's the best sister ever," Viv said right after Griff heard the back door slam. "The very, very best."

"I see that," Griff agreed, slapping another gloppy rectangle of newspaper on his balloon and smoothing it down with his fingers.

"Do you have any siblings?" Vivian asked, her tone conversational. "Roll your balloon over. You missed a spot."

"I haven't gotten to that part yet," he informed her. "And, no, I don't have any brothers or sisters."

Thankfully, no one else besides him had had to endure what he'd had to face as a child. If he'd had to look after a sibling, he didn't know how he would have made it. He'd barely been able to take care of himself.

"Ugh," he groaned as a glop of homemade glue escaped the slip of newspaper he was holding and dropped onto his blue jeans. He wiped at the lumpy white goo with the back of his hand but only succeeded in smearing it across the front of his thigh. "Yuck. Does this stuff wash off?"

Vivian giggled. "Don't worry, sweetie. A little dish soap and water will take it right out."

"Ah. Good." He glanced up to find Vivian staring at him with an odd, inquisitive expression on her face.

His skin prickled and he was suddenly uncomfortable sitting here with Viv, even if she was the girlfriend of his best buddy. He'd seen that look before—on people who'd wanted something from him, usually having to do with money.

What was this?

"So has she managed to butter you up yet?" Viv suddenly blurted, then followed her question with a giggle that set Griff's nerves on edge.

"I'm sorry?" Griff's eyebrows rose and a knot formed in the pit of his stomach. *Please don't let her be talking about Alexis.*

"Alexis," Vivian confirmed with a wide, deceptively innocent grin.

The chains in Griff's gut tightened painfully. "Alexis…what?" he asked cautiously. He didn't want to hear this. He had the sudden urge to stand and walk out of the room before she could say another word. And yet he stayed.

"Has she convinced you to champion her cause yet? You know you can help her, Griff. She's struggling with all that financial stuff having to do with the ranch, right? You're the man when it comes to that kind of thing.

"And think about me, too, while you're at it—and my plans for the spa. Don't you feel just a little bit sorry for me? You kind of just walked away and left me hanging, you know, after you'd promised to help me." She dropped her gaze from his and made a big deal of picking up her papier-mâché balloon and surveying it for any open patches she might have missed.

"Is that what she's been trying to do?" Griff's voice was low and guttural. Nausea rolled over him in waves. "Butter me up?"

"Well, nothing as overt as all that," Vivian clarified with a chuckle. "You know Alexis. She would never come right out and ask for something she needed. She's pretty hush-hush about her problems. But still…"

But still, indeed.

He'd been so certain Alexis was different. The only help she'd ever asked from him was in regard to the teenagers. Was it all a ploy to engage his emotions so he would use his skills to bail her out of her problems? Had she been manipulating him from the start?

"Griff?" Alexis was standing in the doorway of the kitchen again. He'd been so lost in thought that he hadn't heard her return. "Is something wrong? You look a little…green around the gills."

He couldn't force himself to meet her gaze. He imagined he looked more red than green, as flushed as he was feeling. Heat coursed through him.

"I—I'm not feeling too well all of a sudden." That, at least, was the plain, honest truth. "I think I need some air. Excuse me."

He bolted to his feet and zigzagged toward the back door, stumbling along as if he were only now learning how to walk.

Alexis was at his side in an instant, linking her arm through his.

"Let me walk you back," she said resolutely. "You really don't look like yourself right now."

He didn't *feel* like himself—or rather, he felt like the very worst version of the man he obviously was—the fellow who could be so easily duped by a pretty face, not just once, but over and over again.

The fool in all his glory.

"No." Griff was insistent. "I don't want your help."

Alexis dropped her arm from his. Were there tears in her eyes?

A woman's fiercest weapon, tears. Wielded well, they had brought many a man stronger than Griff to his knees.

But Alexis's tears weren't falling. They merely glimmered from the corners of her eyes, her gaze filled with sympathy and—something else. If he didn't know better, he would almost believe he had hurt her feelings.

Almost.

He escaped through the door and didn't look back.

* * *

Griff prided himself on his ability to sleep like a rock no matter what his circumstances. However bad things got for him, he could always find some solace in sleep.

Until last night.

After leaving Alexis and Vivian to their piñata making and devious scheming, he'd headed straight for the bunkhouse and his bed, but sleep had eluded him no matter what he did. He'd tossed and turned the whole night through. The few times he'd drifted off, he would awake in a panic, his heart thundering and every nerve pricked as if by a knife, yet he was unable to remember what he'd been dreaming about.

And then his mind would flood with thoughts of Alexis—her smile, her laugh, her tears. The love and joy in her gaze when she was working with "her" teenagers. How she'd reached out to him when she had every right to send him packing.

Hers wasn't the face of someone who used people for their own benefit. Quite the opposite. She was a giver.

She was straightforward in all her dealings. If she was after his expertise, all she had to do was ask.

But she hadn't. In her independence, she'd not even sought the help of the community around her. He doubted even Viv knew of the silent desperation Alexis hid behind her ready smile.

Alexis was not Caro.

And Griff wasn't the same man he'd been when he'd first arrived in Serendipity. The place had changed him somehow.

Griff rolled to a sitting position on his bed and

draped his legs over the edge. He scrubbed a hand down his face to wipe away the lingering effects of his poor night's sleep and stretched his tired muscles.

After being long conned by Caro, he'd chosen to walk away from the life he'd made for himself. Run, more like it. It had taken that kind of disaster to make him realize he wasn't happy with his life the way it was, with the career he'd chosen and the crooked path he was on. He'd been traveling on cruise control for so long that he no longer knew where he was going.

Who knew how long, if ever, it would have been before he would have taken the time to seriously evaluate his life and make the necessary course corrections?

His heart lodged solidly in his throat as he finally acknowledged a fact that had heretofore eluded him.

As horrible as the experience with Caro had been, perhaps it had all been for the best. Because without that, he wouldn't have come to Serendipity…where he was happy.

Thanks in part to Alexis, he was finally living his life to the hilt. The kids. The horses. The land. The community.

Alexis.

For maybe the first time in his life, he was starting to feel a little less guarded, physically and emotionally.

He might not be ready to knock all his walls down quite yet, but they were definitely starting to crumble.

He couldn't go backward. He wouldn't lose the rare gift that had been given him. Maybe Alexis was the woman he believed she was. Maybe she wasn't. There was one way to know for sure. It wasn't by hiding from the truth, and it most definitely wasn't by running away from it.

Fear and doubt were knocking. Maybe it was time to open the door.

Chapter Seven

Alexis wasn't sure she would see Griff at the party. Something serious had transpired between Vivian and Griff when she'd stepped out to speak to her counselors the night before. Whatever had happened had set him off big time.

Of course, Vivian couldn't give her anything useful. She was absolutely clueless as to what was up with Griff. When Alexis had pressed her, Vivian had burst into tears and it had taken Alexis twenty minutes just to calm her down. Whatever had happened, Alexis was certain Vivian hadn't purposefully meant to say anything upsetting. She had too sensitive a heart to cause such trouble. Silly, maybe, but sensitive all the same.

Alexis would have to turn to Griff for answers, but he'd made it clear that she wasn't welcome around him at the moment, and she wasn't going to chase him. When he was ready, he'd come to her. She just didn't expect it to be anytime soon.

But that was just as well, since she had a party to prepare for and six youth currently waiting on her direction.

"Girls, can you take out all of the plates, cups and plastic silverware and arrange them on one of the tables outside? Somewhere in the boxes you'll find a couple of festive tablecloths—one for the food table and one for the gift table. And feel free to use crepe paper and whatever else you need to decorate. I can't wait to see what your creative minds will do."

The three girls giggled in anticipation and immediately started exploring the contents of the boxes, exclaiming to one another when they found something they could use to decorate for the party.

"Guys, I need your superior height to help me hang crepe paper and banners. There are a couple of footstools in the storage closet."

Connor and Josh raced for the closet, leaving Devon standing alone beside Alexis. He no longer held back as much as he had when he'd first arrived, but Alexis knew she still had a way to go to instill the self-confidence and personal courage she wanted him to possess in his heart by the time he left Redemption Ranch.

"Connor," she said as the two boys returned, "why don't you and Devon go hang that welcome banner across the front porch?"

"Hey, what about me?" Josh protested.

Alexis chuckled. "I need you to help me blow up some balloons."

"Yeah," Josh agreed, grinning and posturing as if he'd won a prize. He punched Connor on the arm. "I don't want to hang out with you losers, anyway."

Alexis arched a brow but didn't comment. She didn't need to. Chagrin immediately covered Josh's face. He was learning the fine line of what was simply harmless teasing and what was hurtful.

Alexis led Josh to the overstuffed blue couch in the living room and reached for a large package of balloons, which she immediately opened, dumping the contents onto the coffee table and tossing a couple into Josh's lap.

She was working on her fifth balloon when she heard voices at the front door. Moments later, Griff entered the house. Despite the fact that she'd told herself she was too busy to worry about him, relief flooded her when she saw that he was here.

If he'd come to help them today, things couldn't be too bad, could they? Maybe she'd imagined the awkwardness of the previous night.

"I saw Devon and Connor outside," he informed her. She read the surprise in his gaze as he took a seat in the armchair across from her. "They were working together—and not fighting. You're not going to believe it, but Devon was even laughing." The way he said the statement, he could have been saying he'd just discovered something as improbable as the moon being made of green cheese.

Alexis chuckled under her breath. How little he knew about her work at the ranch. *Amazing* was just around every corner.

Without waiting to be asked, he grabbed a handful of balloons from the table and put one to his lips. "I definitely have enough hot air to contribute to this endeavor," he commented between breaths.

Alexis's eyes widened, but he just smiled at her and tied his balloon off, then playfully bumped it with his palm, sending it into her lap.

So that was it, then? Crisis averted? Night and day emotions? She scoffed internally. And men said women were confusing.

She tilted her head and flashed him an impish smile, then pushed the balloon back at him. She'd play along, but if he thought he could just brush off what had happened last night without an explanation, he had another think coming.

"Josh, can you start hanging the balloons?" she asked, handing the boy a roll of packing tape. "Anywhere you think looks good, okay? Griff and I will stay here and blow up a few more for you."

Josh trekked off to follow her instructions. Alexis leaned back into the cushion and crossed her arms, settling her gaze on Griff.

At first he didn't appear to notice that she wasn't blowing up a balloon, keeping her full attention on him instead, but eventually he set his balloon aside and faced her.

"What?" he asked warily.

"That was going to be my question to you—as in, what happened last night? I've got to be honest with you and admit I didn't expect you to show up right now."

"Neither did I."

So she was right about him having some kind of problem. For some reason she was relieved by that confirmation. "But?"

"But I took Hercules for a ride this morning to clear my head. I guess I figured out what was bothering me, and I knew I eventually needed to seek you out and talk to you. So here I am."

"Here *I* am," she encouraged. If he'd figured out

what was bothering him, she definitely wanted to know, and she knew it wasn't easy for him to come clean with her this way. "Speak to me."

He fidgeted and combed his fingers through his hair. Josh returned for more balloons and the silence lengthened between them.

"I can't help you if I don't know what's wrong," she reminded him.

Griff cleared his throat and leaned his forearms on his knees, his look determined. "A lot of—" he hesitated "—bad stuff happened to me before I came here. Viv accidentally said something that set me off. That's all it was, and I apologize."

Alexis stood and offered her hand. "Come on. Let's walk."

"But your party," he protested.

"Is perfectly under control. The kids are doing a fine job of decorating, and Vivian can direct them if necessary. We've got some time."

Alexis led Griff away from the house and down the driveway, which would soon be crowded with cars. Halfway down the drive she cut to the side and headed out into the long grass. She could have dropped his hand at that point, and maybe she should have, but she didn't, and neither did he. There was a measure of comfort in the way his large, warm hand enveloped hers. Breaking physical contact would be like breaking the thin thread of understanding between them.

She waited for him to lead the conversation. She could feel the tension rippling through his muscles and knew how difficult it was for him to be out here with her now.

"Vivian didn't mean to upset you, you know," she

finally commented when he continued to walk in strained silence.

"I know." Griff led her to a fallen log and gestured for her to sit. He followed suit and then leaned forward and plucked a tall blade of grass, twisting it into tight knots with his fingers. "Ugh. I'm embarrassed to be talking about this," he admitted in a gruff whisper. "It's humiliating."

"I don't want you to feel uncomfortable," she responded softly. "You can say anything to me. I promise I won't judge."

His gray-blue eyes snapped to hers. "No, I know you won't."

Her breath caught in her throat. His eyes were full of a rampage of emotion and Alexis's heart swelled with compassion and something else she wasn't quite ready to identify. "I'm ready to listen to whatever you have to say."

He crooked his leg and turned toward her. "When I came here—to Serendipity, to Redemption Ranch—I was running away from a bad relationship."

Sympathy washed over her. She could see his heartbreak in his eyes. She could feel it in her own heart. "I'm so sorry. Vivian mentioned that you had recently had your heart broken. I hope it's okay that she shared that with me."

"Had my heart broken?" he repeated. "Yeah. I guess that's how it felt at the time. But now that I have a little distance from what happened, I think mostly Caro just injured my pride. I've always been self-sufficient. Maybe too much so."

Alexis smiled softly. "I can relate."

"Yes, well, you're considerably wiser than me. You

like to handle your problems yourself, but that doesn't mean you close yourself off from people. I didn't have the greatest experiences growing up and I managed to build a pretty solid wall around myself."

"You see yourself in Devon."

His breath caught audibly and he released it slowly. "Yes. I do."

"That explains a lot."

"But not why I act so out of sorts sometimes. You said I got my heart broken, and that's partially true. I had my bubble burst, is more like it. You see, I'm a self-made man. Everything I accomplished as an adult I did completely of my own volition, through my own hard work."

"And with God's blessing," she added.

"God? No, I don't think God ever had much use for me."

Alexis squeezed his hand. "I disagree. But now is not the time for a sermon. Please continue."

"I started dabbling in high society in Houston— rubbing elbows with people with money, power and prestige. Ruthless people, for the most part. I thought I wanted to be like them."

"You wanted to be accepted." Alexis's heart was overflowing with emotion. It was all she could do not to burst into tears, but she suspected that a sobbing female was the last thing Griff needed right now. It might even drive him away, and she couldn't bear to be this close to finally discovering more about who Griff really was to ruin it by her inability to keep her feelings to herself.

"What? No. I don't care if I'm accepted. I mean—" He paused and his gaze widened. "You may be right," he acknowledged gravely. "Maybe that was what I was looking for and just didn't want to admit it. In any case, I was—not happy, but satisfied, pursuing my business interests and making conquests, at least until the day Caro Masterson called me. At first she was just asking advice about a charity she was involved with. But the more we talked, the closer we became. We eventually met in person. I ended up funneling a lot of my own personal money into her *charity*. It got personal—at least, for me, it did."

"She didn't feel the same way?" she asked, even though she already knew the answer to her question.

He snorted in derision. "She wasn't even a single woman. She was married. And her charity was a scam. As it turned out, she and her husband were embezzling the money and cooking the books."

"Oh, my." Alexis's heart was breaking for him and all he'd endured. No wonder he was cautious of her and of Redemption Ranch. Why wouldn't he be? He had every right not to trust a charity, or a woman, for that matter.

"What can I say? I'm a chump."

"No, you're not. Please don't call yourself names. Don't you see? You were targeted. You can't blame yourself for what happened."

His lips twisted. "Can't I? I fell for it hook, line and sinker. And by the time I'd figured out I'd been scammed, Caro and her husband had skipped town."

"Along with your money."

He shrugged. "The money doesn't matter."

"Of course not. It's what she did to your heart that counts."

"My heart?" He shook his head. "I'm not even sure

I have a heart. I definitely still struggle with trust, even when it's been more than earned. Yet the second your sister goes and mentions that she needs help with her spa and that you are having financial problems with your ministry, I go ballistic."

"Me? She said *I* needed your help?" No wonder Griff had gone off the deep end. Vivian and her big mouth. "Where did she come up with that notion? Griff, I'm not asking anything of you. I never even thought about it, I promise you that."

"Yeah. I know. Once I calmed down, I thought back over the time we've spent together here at the ranch and I realized that if you were setting out to con me, you were doing a pretty poor job of it. You never asked me for a thing, and I don't believe you've ever mentioned Vivian's spa."

Heat rose to Alexis's face. "I have to be totally honest with you. She did talk to me about putting a bug in your ear regarding her business, but I promise you she meant no harm by it. I feel terrible that she even brought it up to you, knowing what I know now."

"Don't. Anyway, she's right. I did leave her hanging. She's my best friend's girl. I told her I'd help—she had every right to count on me, and yet I didn't even bother to finish what I started for her. I'm surprised she's even speaking to me, after the way I bailed on her."

"Vivian doesn't hold grudges."

"No, she certainly doesn't. But I feel bad even so. I'll make it right by her," he vowed. "First thing Monday morning, I'll make some calls and get her spa properly funded. She has a solid business plan and it won't take much to get investors interested."

"Thank you. She may have gone about it the wrong

way, but I know she would never purposefully hurt you. Not for the world. You have to understand that her spa is her heart's desire, what she's wanted to do ever since she was a little girl."

"I've learned a little something about dreams," Griff said, "especially after coming here. People should pursue their heart's desire instead of just trudging along, bowing to the almighty dollar. If opening her spa will make her happy, I'm glad to help her." He glanced at his watch, then up at Alexis, smiling crookedly. "It's nearly five o'clock. We ought to get back, don't you think? I'm sure your guests don't want to miss congratulating the birthday girl."

Alexis rolled her eyes and sighed dramatically. "Don't remind me. The things I do for my sister."

Griff stood and reached out both hands to assist Alexis to her feet. "The things you do for everybody."

Griff didn't know what he expected from a small-town birthday party, but one thing was for certain—Alexis and Vivian had lots of friends. The house was so packed that there was barely any elbow room to move. The crowd had overflowed outside, where a couple of local men were busy grilling hot dogs and hamburgers.

He'd lost track of Alexis somewhere along the way. She was busy playing hostess to her dozens of guests. He hadn't wanted to follow her around like a lost puppy dog, so he'd made his way indoors and had found a wall to hold up.

He didn't mind being alone and was content to watch the flood of locals chatting away while their children dashed around screeching in delight. His heart felt lighter than it had felt in years. Maybe ever. He hadn't realized what a heavy burden he'd been carrying around, or that it was as simple as taking advantage of the ear and heart of a compassionate woman to unload that unwelcome encumbrance.

"Hey, Griff, remember me?" The sheriff who'd demonstrated K9 tactics to Alexis's teens heartily shook Griff's hand.

"Eli, is it?"

"Yes, sir. What do you think of the birthday bash? Tamer than what you're used to, I would imagine."

"Tamer? Try wilder, by a long shot." Griff laughed. "I've never been to a party that had so many kids running around."

Eli grinned and nodded. "Yep, there is that. Never a dull moment around here. Loud and boisterous. You'd think a small town would be all quiet and peaceful, right?"

Griff chuckled. If he'd known how active and close-knit the Serendipity community was before he'd come, he would have talked himself out of it.

"How is your search for land going? Have you found any good prospects yet? Jo mentioned your plan to settle here."

"That's the idea." Now, more than ever. "But to be honest, I've been kind of caught up in all the goings-on here at Redemption Ranch. It's a busy place. I regret to say I haven't done much scouting of the area yet."

Eli chuckled. "Don't worry. You won't have to do any of the work. The folks here in town know of your need. Your land will come to you, handed to you on a silver platter. Just you wait and watch." He slapped Griff on the back. "What do you say we go find Alexis? If I don't miss my guess, my wife will be right by her side, along with Samantha, of course. The Little Chicks."

"I've heard the story about that nickname."

"Trust me, they've earned it."

Griff tried to follow Eli out of the crowded house, but every couple of feet he was stopped by another one of the locals. Everyone seemed to know who he was and what he was looking for, real-estate wise. In the short distance from the living room to the front yard, he managed to receive several solid leads on land he planned to follow up on.

After some minutes speaking with his new neighbors, he finally made it outside. Like a magnet, his gaze captured Alexis's. She was standing between the two grills, serving hamburgers. Eli had called it correctly—Mary and a dark-haired woman Griff assumed was Samantha hovered nearby, chattering like the little chicks they were, even as they helped Alexis serve food to her guests. Griff chuckled. He had to admit they did rather sound like a flock of very cheerful birds.

He started to approach and then stopped suddenly when he spotted a large table set up under an oak tree. The table was laden with enormous piles of prettily wrapped presents with elaborate bows and an assortment of colorful gift bags.

Presents.

He wanted to smack himself upside the head. It was their *birthday,* for crying out loud. How dim-witted was he? As wrapped up as he'd been in his own problems, it hadn't even occurred to him to buy Alexis and Vivian gifts. He'd known there would be a party. Parties meant gifts. Some houseguest he was.

At this time of night, especially on a Saturday, the

whole town would be locked up as tight as a safe. Most likely, everyone who worked on Main Street was here at the party. It hadn't taken Griff more than a few days to discover that particular idiosyncrasy of small-town living.

But that fact put him in an impossible position. No twenty-four-hour drugstore on the corner. No shopping mall down the street. No possible way to sneak off and come back bearing gifts.

"You look as if you just swallowed a lemon, son." Griff hadn't even realized Jo Spencer had approached him until she followed her words with a playful slap on the biceps. "What's troubling you, dear?"

Griff lifted his gray cowboy hat and scrubbed his fingers through his hair, shook his head and scoffed. "I'm an idiot, that's what. Ugh."

Jo burst into such earsplitting boisterous laughter that a few people turned to look their direction.

"Now, I'm not sayin' you are, and I'm not sayin' you ain't, but why don't you tell me what happened and let me be the judge. Just what did you do?"

Griff groaned. "It's not what I did, Jo. It's what I didn't do—as in purchase gifts for Alexis and Vivian. I feel terrible."

"Oh, now, honey, don't you worry none about those two. As you can see, they've already got themselves more gifts than they're gonna know what to do with. I'm sure they're just pleased you're here to help them celebrate their happy day. Good folks is more important than pretty presents. That's the kind of women they are."

"I know. That's exactly it. That's why I'm so determined to get them something, although at this point it's going to be belated. They've already done so much for me. I can't even measure it all. I only wish—"

Griff's breath slammed to a halt in his chest as an idea bucked him right out of the saddle and sent him tumbling to the earth.

"I can do something for them," he muttered, more to himself than to Jo, as the lightbulb in his head sparked and flared.

"Well, of course you can, dear." Jo stared at him intently for a moment and then linked her arm with his. "I see the wheels turning in your head. You've got a plan, Griff Haddon. Share and share alike, I always say."

He wasn't going to get out of this one anytime soon. May as well play along.

Griff quirked a smile and his eyebrows danced. "I'm not sure I ought to say, seeing as your shirt reads One for You, Two for Me."

"Oh, you," Jo said, followed by a shrill cackle. "You don't have to worry about me takin' the credit for your ideas."

The lightbulb in his head flared again, even brighter this time. His pulse hammered as he remembered all the friendly faces he'd met even just today. Everyone seemed ready and willing to help him, a stranger in town. How much more would they respond to the needs of one of their own?

"Actually, Jo, that's exactly what I want you to do."

Her face crinkled in confusion. "I'm not sure I'm following, son."

"I'm looking for investors to back a worthy project."

A smile burst onto her lips with such ferocity that her whole face beamed like the sun's rays. "Why, you're speaking of Redemption Ranch."

Griff tipped his hat with his thumb and forefinger. "Yes, ma'am. Redemption Ranch."

"We're a humble village with modest means. Unfortunately there aren't many in our community who can afford as big a chunk of change as investing requires, even for so good a cause as this."

"Maybe not," Griff agreed. "But a whole lot of folks offering what they can, sharing even a tiny bit of their abundance, adds up the same way one or two deep-pocketed investors would. Don't you think?"

"I like your math, young man."

"So you'll help me, then?" Anticipation and exhilaration coursed through him. "I don't mind doing the legwork and I'll definitely be the one to solicit funds, but I'd appreciate any introductions you can offer."

"Consider me your right-hand woman. I happen to sit on the board for Redemption Ranch. I'll contact the other board members and let them know where we're thinking of going with this. Come see me at the café on Monday and we'll work out our strategy."

A step beyond the exhilaration, Griff felt a moment's panic. What was he doing? Exactly what he'd sworn he'd never do—help another woman in distress. He was running, not walking, down the path of potential destruction.

He believed in Alexis. He did. But that didn't stop the doubt from looming like a dark shadow in his mind. Not doubt in her, but in himself. Would he get in over his head again, lose perspective as he had before? Caro had set out to trick him in a way that Alexis never would—but still, he'd be putting himself out there becoming this invested in the project. And doing that opened him up to getting hurt.

He forced a smile. "Yes, ma'am. Will do. I'm anxious to get started. Oh—and, Jo. One more thing, if you don't mind?"

"What's that, dear?"

The one thing he could still do to shelter his heart. "I'd prefer that Alexis not be aware of my involvement in this project at this stage of the process."

"Now, how's she gonna know it's your gift to her if she ain't aware of who's doin' it for her?"

"Right. Good point. But I have my reasons—good ones." He tensed, his jaw tightening, as he waited for her to press him.

Her wide-eyed stare penetrated his, disconcerting him. It was almost as if she could tell what he was thinking without him saying anything out loud. He barely restrained himself from fidgeting on the balls of his feet.

"Good enough for me," she said with a definitive nod.

Relief flooded through him at the realization that she wasn't going to push him on the issue. He wasn't ready to disclose his past to anyone but Alexis. Ironically enough, it was Alexis who would most understand his reluctance to reveal his involvement in this arrangement. And how crazy was that?

"Griff?"

He returned his attention to the older woman, half afraid she'd changed her mind and would push him for more information. But she just smiled up at him and gently patted his cheek.

"I'm proud of you, dear."

She turned and walked away before he could respond, which was probably a good thing, because he couldn't have said anything to save his life. His face was flushed and he was too choked up for words.

No one had ever said they were proud of him before.

As he was struggling to contain the unfamiliar deluge of emotions flaring through him, Vivian danced past him. He snaked out an arm to grab her elbow.

"Griff!" she exclaimed with a sincere smile. "Isn't this wonderful? Are you enjoying my party?"

He chuckled. She really didn't hold grudges. There wasn't even the hint of accusation in her gaze.

"I am. Happy birthday, Viv."

Her eyes glowed. Once again Griff was struck by how much different Viv looked to him than Alexis. Funny how that was; his intimate familiarity with the twins. It was totally disconcerting to realize he had a strong preference for one of the women—he would rather be looking into Alexis's eyes than Viv's.

"I have a gift for you." He dangled the words like a carrot, knowing Viv would bite. "But it's not something I can wrap."

Vivian squealed in delight and clapped her hands, reminding Griff of an overexcited toddler. "Tell me. Tell me."

Her enthusiasm rubbed off on him. "Hmm. You're sure you want to know? Because I can keep it a secret."

She grabbed at his collar. "Spill it, mister."

"Hey." Griff was surprised to hear Alexis's voice coming from behind him. "I don't want to see you manhandling my houseguest."

Griff's heart thumped so heavily he thought the twins might be able to hear it. Alexis had referred to him as *her* guest, not *their* guest. It probably meant nothing to her, but it meant something to him. He turned to include Alexis in their little group.

"I was just wishing Vivian a happy birthday. Same to you, Alexis."

"He mentioned a *gift,*" Vivian added eagerly. "And he was about to tell me what it was when we were so rudely interrupted."

"Please don't let me stop you," Alexis said with a laugh.

Griff winked at Alexis. "I was just about to tell her that I'm planning to secure the investors she needs to complete her financing. You can build your spa, Vivian."

Vivian squealed and hugged Griff, then dashed off through the crowd to share her good news with her friends.

Griff chuckled and turned toward Alexis. "That went well, I think."

"Oh, Griff." Alexis sniffed and blinked rapidly. Griff was surprised to see her beautiful blue eyes brimming with tears. "You do realize you just gave Vivian her best birthday present ever. I'm talking, like, the best gift of her whole life. You blessed her with the answer to her prayers."

Seeing Alexis's tears made Griff's gut tighten into knots. He fervently wished he could bless Alexis with the answer to *her* prayers, as she had so eloquently phrased it. But he couldn't, at least not yet. He wasn't even completely certain he'd be successful at all in the plan he'd constructed. If his idea fell through, it would be back to the drawing board. And even if it all worked out, he'd never dare term it an answer to a prayer.

But what if he failed? What would Alexis do then?

As far as he was aware, her business plan was non-existent and the investment capitalists he'd worked with in the past wanted to see profit. Success measured in the reformation of teenage delinquents didn't make for a noteworthy bottom line for men such as that.

No, he had to make *this* plan work—helping the community embrace her and her ministry. He just had to. But in the meantime, Alexis was crying and he had no immediate gift to make her feel better.

"Hey, I'm sorry," he murmured, pulling her into his arms despite the fact there was a crowd around them.

"For what?" Her voice was muffled in the cotton of his shirt.

"I feel like an oaf. I just gave Vivian a present of sorts, but I'm ashamed to say I didn't get you anything."

"Are you kidding me?" she exclaimed, leaning back just enough for her eyes to meet his. Her arms were still firmly wrapped around his waist. "You've given me the most precious gift ever—the look of joy in my sister's eyes. These are happy tears, Griff. You have to understand. Viv and I have both worked and struggled so that she could pursue her dreams. You're the answer to my prayers, too, Griff Haddon."

She hugged him so tight she pressed the air from his lungs. But it didn't matter. It wasn't as if he would have been able to breathe, anyway.

He'd never been the answer to anyone's prayer before.

Chapter Eight

Alexis closed her checkbook ledger and pushed it to the side with a sigh that was a mixture of regret and relief. She'd paid everyone's salaries until the end of the month and as many bills as her meager bank account would allow.

For the millionth time she wished things were different, that she could continue running Redemption Ranch and concentrate on what she could and did do for the teenagers, rather than how far she would be able to stretch every dollar. She wished she could hire an accountant, or at least an administrative assistant to help her manage all of her paperwork. How ironic was it that the very reason she couldn't hire someone to manage her money was that she had no money to manage.

She wasn't a corporation or a large ministry. With only the friends and neighbors on her little board of directors to guide her, she felt alone with her goals and dreams, all of which were about to fade into the sunset. She was proud of what she'd done, but there was still so much she wished she could do—so many thoughts and plans that would now never be brought to life.

The craziest thought of all was in regard to Griff Haddon. Because if Redemption Ranch was a triumphant success instead of an unmitigated disaster, she would seriously be thinking about offering Griff a position at the ranch.

That was a ridiculous notion on any number of levels. First of all, as far as she knew, he was rich as Midas. He didn't need a job. He had plans that didn't include her or the ranch. He'd told her straight out that he didn't especially like teenagers. And she didn't have a specific position in mind for him, even if she had the money to offer him something.

Which of course she didn't.

She sighed and cupped her face in her palms as her mind drifted to her handsome houseguest. She simply couldn't shake the feeling that he belonged here. He was so good with her kids. Not just Devon, although he'd certainly reached that young man in a special way. But the way that he'd rallied all the teenagers after the party and had convinced them to work together to clean up the mess was nothing if not remarkable. He was a natural leader who was able to motivate the kids without ever being condescending or talking down to them—a rare and special skill.

He'd plunked Alexis and Vivian into armchairs and hadn't let them get up even to refill their own drinks. They were strictly ordered to put up their feet and relax. Griff and the teens had done everything for them. There wasn't a single dirty dish or crumpled napkin for her to care for after they'd finished.

There was much to admire in a man like Griff. From what she gathered, he'd endured some sort of traumatic childhood, and yet had the strength of will to rise above it, to become his own man and, best of all, to recognize that making money wasn't the be all and end all of a productive life.

She was proud of him for the man he was becoming. And yes, she couldn't deny it, she was attracted to Griff in a way she'd never been attracted to another man. When their eyes met, when their hands touched, she felt as if she was walking on clouds, yet at the same time, she was energized in a way she couldn't explain in words.

Wouldn't Vivian have a good laugh if she realized just how effective her little matchmaking ploy had been? In one of her typical crazy schemes, she'd sent Alexis a man out of the blue, not knowing that she and Griff would have a physical and emotional chemistry that registered off the charts.

But she wasn't in a position to get serious about a man. Her life was in shambles and troubles were raining down all around her. How could she even consider burdening Griff with the fallout of her failed ministry? The man was looking to get away from toil and turmoil, not dive into the middle of someone else's mire.

Peace and quiet she could not give him. Welcome to her chaos.

And if that wasn't enough, he had other issues he was dealing with. The Lord was working on his heart. She could see it in the way his attitude toward the teenagers had changed, and how active he'd been visiting with her friends and neighbors at her party. Griff was learning to love—not only others, but himself. She prayed every day that this new openness would extend even further—upward. She firmly believed that it wouldn't be long before Griff finally became aware of the love God had for him.

She needed to stay out of God's way and allow Him to work in His own good time. She had a bad habit of interfering, and it wasn't up to her. Just as with her beloved teenagers, her part was to show God's love in her words and actions and then step back and watch the Lord at work in their lives.

She was startled half out of her wits when Griff suddenly appeared in the door of her office. He looked like a regular native in scuffed boots and blue jeans, his gray cowboy hat curled in his hand.

"I knocked but no one answered. I hope it's okay that I let myself in. I figured I might find you working in here."

"Praying, more like," she admitted with a dry chuckle. "I'm not sure working is going to help me at this point. Come on in."

Griff sank into the chair opposite her. "Any lightning bolts from God? Money raining from the sky?"

"Hmm. I wish. No such luck. Not today, anyway. Was there a reason you needed to see me?"

"Just to ask if it would be okay if I took Hercules out for a ride. He and I have kind of bonded. I thought since I have a little free time this afternoon I would pretend to be a cowboy for a while."

"You don't have to pretend, Griff. I've seen you in the saddle. You have as natural a seat as most of the men who've grown up out here in the country."

His face brightened. "You think?"

"Absolutely. And I'm glad you picked Hercules. He doesn't get as much attention as some of the other mounts do. I can't put a completely inexperienced rider on him, which of course most of my teenagers are. Hercules has a mind of his own, and he can be a bit skittish, as I'm sure you're aware."

Griff chuckled. "That's what makes him fun."

Why was she not surprised that docile wasn't Griff's style? "You might run across the teens and the wranglers while you're out there. If I'm not mistaken, they're out mending fences today."

"That never ceases to amaze me."

"What's that?"

"How you've taken the kids and turned them around." He shook his head and grunted softly. "I remember how unruly they were at their first dinner with you. Now they're out there mending your fences, and probably enjoying every minute of it, too."

Alexis choked on a laugh. "Them? I seem to remember how unruly *you* were at that first dinner."

Griff had the good grace to blush. "Touché."

"You've improved some upon acquaintance." Her lips quirked.

He smiled crookedly and tilted his head, his gaze warm and inviting. "You haven't."

"Well, thank you very much for that," she quipped back at him. The way he was looking at her was causing her stomach to do all kinds of crazy somersaults.

"And by that," he drawled lightly, "I mean you were already perfect then, just as you are now. There's no room for improvement where you're concerned."

"Oh, you!" Her mind flashed to her disastrous relationship with paperwork and fund-raising—both of which he knew about.

He thought she was perfect? The man was blind as a bat.

"Flattery, my dear man, will get you everywhere."

"Is that so? I'll have to keep that in mind." He planted his cowboy hat on his head and straightened the brim.

"Don't get lost," she teased.

He winked. "Same to you. I know from experience how massive piles of paperwork can bury a person."

Alexis brushed her hair back behind her ear as she watched Griff walk away. "I won't," she murmured belatedly.

Even as she said it, she knew it wasn't quite true. She *was* getting lost, but it wasn't the paperwork she was worried about.

What concerned her was that she might be losing her heart.

This was the life.

Griff pulled in a deep, cleansing breath, full of the heady scent of horse and leather. He relished his boots in the stirrups, the feel of the thick leather reins threaded between his fingers. The strength of Hercules's stride as the bay quarter horse loped across the fields. The sun in his face and the brush of the wind in his hair. The fresh air expanding his lungs as he leisurely explored acres of peaceful grassland.

Truly, this was the life. That this was the potential of what his life was going to be like from here on out exhilarated him in a way no business deal had ever done. Even the most challenging and rewarding contracts left a bad taste in his mouth compared to the peace and contentment he was now experiencing. The only thing he would miss about his previous life was the chance to help people with his funding and experience—but he had the chance to do that here, too.

After this morning's meeting with Jo at the café, he was feeling even more motivated and encouraged. He'd known from the moment he'd met her that she would be a good person to have in his corner, but he'd had no idea what a shrewd businesswoman's mind lurked underneath all that curly red hair. Jo had given a lot of thought to their strategy and already had a contact list squarely in place. She'd not only collected a prioritized list of names and numbers, but had provided the kind of practical and personal information about the folks on the list that he wouldn't have been able to purchase from the most elaborate of data brokers— such as how each person or family knew Alexis and why they would be personally interested in helping her out. Thanks to Jo, he was loaded for bear and had a new sense of confidence that this small-town investor scenario would work.

Wouldn't Alexis be surprised to discover she wouldn't have to set aside her dreams for the ranch? Oh, to see her face when he told her the good news.

Wait.

His heart dropped into the pit of his stomach as he realized he probably wasn't going to be the one to tell her. His sense of elation dissipated like the morning dew. It was very likely he wouldn't be there at all. It would probably be Jo Spencer breaking the news to her, just as they had discussed at Alexis's and Vivian's birthday party.

It wasn't as though he was going to be living at Redemption Ranch forever. As much as he'd come to appreciate this place and the woman who owned it, Alexis was expecting him to move on as soon as he could secure a place of his own. And rightly so. He'd taken advantage of her good graces for long enough as it was. He still wasn't fully ready to put his heart on the line again—and the more time he spent with Alexis, the greater the risk for losing it entirely.

No, the credit for supporting Alexis in her worthwhile ministry would go to those to whom it truly belonged—the community that loved her and would stand by her even when he could not. It wouldn't be right for him to press his own advantage.

Arriving back at the stable, Griff guided Hercules into the corral and dismounted, loosening the girth and sliding the reins over the horse's head.

"I've got a bucket of grain waiting for you, boy," he informed the horse as he led Hercules into the stall. "Let's get you rubbed down and then I'll give you your special treat. You worked hard today. You deserve it, right?"

He'd unsaddled Hercules and was reaching for a currycomb when he heard a sound that was completely at odds with the peace and quiet of the stable.

Someone was crying.

At first it was so low Griff thought he might have imagined it. He froze, straining his ears to decipher where the sound had come from—or if it existed at all.

There it was again. Muffled, but definitely the sound of weeping.

"Hello?" he called, his voice echoing off the stable walls. "Who is it? Do you need some help?"

His questions met with total silence as the sobs abruptly cut off.

"It's Griff Haddon," he gently informed his invisible company. He stepped out of Hercules's stall and started slowly walking the length of the stable, peering over each of the stall doors.

He heard a sniffle just as he reached Pitonio's stall.

"Devon?" Pitonio thrust his nose forward and bumped Griff's arm, shifting sideways just enough for Griff to spy the ink-haired young man slumped in the back corner, wrapped in his trench coat with his head buried in his arms. His shoulders were quivering but no sound emerged.

Griff gripped the top of the stall door and fought the tidal waves of emotion surging through him.

Anger. Fear. Anxiety.

He wasn't just experiencing memories of the many emotions he'd experienced as a teenager. He was feeling what Devon felt. It was almost as if the young man was projecting *his* emotions on to Griff. The effect was startling, to say the least.

"Hey there, Dev," he greeted, speaking in as gentle a tone as he would with a spooked horse.

"Go away," Devon replied in a shaky, gravelly voice. He didn't even bother to lift his head from his arms.

Griff only hesitated for a moment before slipping into the stall and pulling the door closed behind him. He slid his hands along Pitonio's flank until the horse shifted enough to allow him access to the trembling young man.

He crouched on the ground next to Devon, not so close as to touch the boy but close enough that his presence would be reassuring. He racked his brain for the right words to say, knowing that blurting out the wrong thing would be worse than remaining silent. It occurred to him too late that maybe he should have gone for help instead of attempting this on his own, but something in his gut compelled him to stay.

"Go away," Devon repeated gruffly.

Griff sat stock-still, staring at the boy and willing him to lift his gaze.

After a moment Devon raised his head and glared at Griff, his dark eyes clouded with pain. "I said, leave me alone."

"I heard you," Griff acknowledged grimly. "And I understand why you think you want to be alone right now. But if you think I'm just gonna walk out of here and leave you to your misery, you don't know me very well, son."

"I'm not your son." Resentment dripped from his voice. He didn't trust Griff, and it was no wonder. Griff guessed the adults in Devon's life hadn't given him much reason to do so, and he knew from experience how that felt. It was no surprise to Griff that Devon had sought refuge in Pitonio's stall. How many times as a teenager had he done the same, hiding out with his neighbor's mustangs? The desire to purchase horses of his own played deeply into his childhood uncertainties.

"You're right," he agreed, casually leaning back, his palms digging into the fresh straw. "You're not my son. But I hope I can be your friend. I'm a good listener, if you want to talk about whatever is bothering you. You can trust me. You won't find any judgment from my quarter."

Devon's breath caught audibly and he looked away. A muscle twitched in the corner of his taut jaw.

"Or we can just sit here." Griff didn't know how far he could push Devon before he would snap, so he mentally backed off a bit and waited for Devon to make the next move. Griff wished Alexis was here with them. She was the empathetic one, the person who always seemed to know the right thing to do or to say to make things better.

All Griff knew was that Devon was fighting—with himself, with the world. Griff knew a little bit about that struggle, but he also knew he couldn't help Devon unless the teenager wanted to be helped.

"I'm not going to make it," Devon groaned.

That was a cry for help if Griff had ever heard one. But what did Devon mean? That sounded ominous, and Griff was more convinced than ever that he was in way over his head. He wasn't qualified to be sitting here advising the boy. Devon sounded as though he was about ready to drown. He needed people trained in dealing with troubled teenagers. He needed counselors.

He needed Alexis.

But it wasn't Alexis or Marcus who'd found Devon. It was Griff. For whatever it was worth, he knew he couldn't just walk away from the situation, especially since Devon was actually speaking to him. Reaching out, in his own way.

As ill-equipped as Griff felt, it was up to him to be there for Devon and to hopefully at least get him to the point where someone with more training could take over.

"This whole experience here at Redemption Ranch is kind of over the top, isn't it?" he asked.

Devon shook his head.

Griff tried again. "Are you still having trouble with the other guys?"

Again, Devon shook his head, but he didn't offer any other clues to what was bothering him.

"Alexis is tough, but she means well," Griff offered. "If you think she's being too hard on you—"

"No!" Devon's shout was adamant, his voice ringing through the stable. "It's not Miss Grainger. She's—" His eyes welled with fresh tears.

If it wasn't the other kids and it wasn't Alexis, what had the boy so depressed?

"She's what?" Griff prompted softly.

Devon wiped his eyes with the corner of his dusty denim shirt. "She loves me," he admitted, his voice low and rough.

"Yeah," Griff agreed. "She does."

Devon shot to his feet and backed into the corner of the stall, crouched in a defensive position, as if someone was coming at him with a knife. "I can't go back," he said, his voice rising in desperation. "Please. Don't make me go back."

"To the ranch house?" Griff was confused.

Devon shook his head in fierce denial. "Home. Don't make me go home. I don't think I can take it."

What Devon asked was impossible. Griff didn't see how that outcome could be avoided. There was only one week left in the Mission Month and then all the kids would return to their daily lives, their debts to society paid and hopefully functioning as better individuals because of their experiences at Redemption Ranch. The other kids, for all that they clearly loved the ranch, seemed to be looking forward to going home. He'd overheard snatches of conversations about plans to sleep in, go shopping, take trips with their families all discussed with obvious enthusiasm.

But Devon—he was as frightened as a field mouse dangling in the jaws of a monster house cat.

Griff's first reaction was to flat-out ask Devon what awaited him at home, but his conscience cautioned against such a forward approach. He remembered his own youth and the resentful young man he had been. He wouldn't have opened up to some guy pushing him to reveal the private and shameful details of his sad excuse for a family life.

Maybe there was another way to approach it.

"When I was your age, I didn't like hanging out at home, either." He hadn't admitted that before. Not out loud. Not to anyone. Even now it pained him to speak of it. But if he could establish some kind of baseline, a common denominator with Devon, maybe the youth would feel comfortable enough to open up to him. "I got kicked around a lot."

Devon slumped back to the ground, glaring at the stall door instead of looking directly at Griff. But at least he wasn't leaving.

"I wasn't big on high school, either, for that matter. I wasn't like the other kids. I was tall and skinny and lived on the wrong side of the tracks. My mom didn't bother getting me new clothes at the beginning of the school year. I wore other men's ill-fitting hand-me-downs, usually from whatever guy was my mom's boyfriend at the time."

Devon grunted noncommittally, but his gaze momentarily slid toward Griff and he saw the flash of interest, and maybe even empathy, in the boy's eyes.

"Yeah. So my mom wasn't the greatest role model. She never had much use for me, I don't think. And I wasn't very good at making friends my own age. I had to find my own way in the world. Alone."

"My mom loved me." Scowling, Devon blew out a frustrated breath and then sniffed loudly.

"I'll bet she did." Griff didn't know what it was like to have a parent who cared for him, and empathy didn't come naturally to him in the best of situations, but he could feel for this young man. Griff was also the product of losing a mother, just not in the way Devon had. At least Devon's mother had loved him. No wonder the boy was devastated. "I'm really sorry for your loss."

"What about your dad?" Devon's voice took on a hard edge, and Griff suddenly realized that was the question *he* should be asking the young man. The key he'd been searching for to unlock the angst in Devon's story had been right in front of him all along.

"I never knew my dad," Griff admitted, surprised by the intensity of the anger that flared up in his chest. He was even more shocked to discover the feeling was directed at his own father and not wholly on what was happening with Devon.

Griff had known he resented the way his mother had blown him off, but he hadn't realized that he harbored latent anger in his heart toward the father he had never known and who had never been a part of his life.

"Your dad left your mom?" Devon asked.

"No. As far as I know, it wasn't like that. I don't think my mother was ever in a real relationship with my father. I'm not even positive she knew for sure who my dad was. My mama didn't live a very…" he paused and scrubbed a hand down his stubbled jaw "…moral life."

And she hadn't taught her son any morals, either. Griff had been floundering around his whole life not even realizing there were absolutes in the world, at least until he had met Alexis. Then he'd discovered that just as he'd always known there was evil in the world, there was likewise some good. As dark as his heart was, Alexis's was every bit as light.

There was hope in this world. He just didn't quite know how to find it, and he definitely didn't know how to communicate it to Devon.

"I wish my mom never knew my dad," Devon admitted. Finally he met Griff's gaze and the anger and pain Griff read there mirrored his own.

"Was he... Is he... That is..." Griff stumbled over his words. "Did he hurt your mother, Devon?" *Did he hurt you?* Griff left the question unspoken but asked it with his eyes.

Devon scowled. "He didn't hit her, if that's what you mean."

That *was* what Griff had meant, but now he realized the ability to hurt someone reached much further than a physical blow. Some of Griff's mother's boyfriends had been downright mean. He'd been beat up more times than he cared to admit, so it was no wonder that's where his conclusions had immediately jumped. Others had found different ways to be cruel, and Griff knew firsthand how badly emotional abuse could hurt.

The pain in Devon's gaze was real, as was his plea not to be returned to his home.

"Tell me about your dad." Griff didn't know the questions to ask. He hoped Devon would offer the missing pieces of the puzzle.

"He's a politician. A state senator."

"So he knows a lot of people. And he gets a lot of respect and attention."

Devon sputtered. "Yeah."

"I suppose most kids would probably think it's pretty cool for you to have a dad in the senate. Someone kind of famous, right?"

Devon nodded miserably.

"But they don't know the truth, do they?" Neither did Griff—yet. But he suspected he was about to find out.

"My dad is gone a lot."

"I'm sorry."

"I'm not. I'm glad when he's gone. I don't like it when he's home. He either yells a lot or ignores me."

"Do you stay with relatives while he's away?"

The youth's brown eyes percolated to black. "No. He won't let me. He pays some old nanny to come in and watch me. I'm too old for a babysitter. Anyway, I'd like to stay with my gran, but he won't let me."

"Why not?"

"Gran is my mom's mom. Dad was so mad at my mom for dying that he won't let me see Gran anymore. I used to go over to her house all the time, and now I'm not allowed to see her at all."

"That's rough."

Devon punched his fist into a nearby hay bale.

Griff wanted to do the same. What was he supposed to do now?

Chapter Nine

Alexis wasn't worried when Devon hadn't showed up for the afternoon board games, even though the rest of her young crew seemed anxious to spend time together. Technically, it was an open afternoon, and Devon had mentioned to Marcus that he'd wanted to save his free time for his horse Pitonio. Devon had really taken to riding, and Alexis thought he was probably enjoying an afternoon hanging out with the wranglers. She believed Devon was getting along better with his peers, but she couldn't fault him for wanting to spend his free time with his new equine friend.

It wasn't until suppertime, when Devon's chair remained empty, that she became anxious. She left the other teens in their counselors' care and set off to see if she could locate Devon herself. She already knew he wasn't in the bunkhouse, because Marcus had just come from there. She visited the wrangler's dwelling, thinking Devon might have decided to chow down with the cowboys, but they hadn't seen the youth all day.

Panic immediately set in. She was responsible for Devon. If he were lost or hurt, that was all on her.

She exited the wrangler's bunkhouse in a rush and headed toward the stable, her legs shaky as she bolted into a dead run.

Please, please, please, Lord, help me find him, she prayed silently as she approached the stable. She wished she had Griff's cell number so she could phone him to see if he'd had any contact with the boy today. If Pitonio wasn't in his stall, she didn't know what she was going to do. She had this awful picture of Devon taking off somewhere on his mount with no intention of returning.

Running away.

Should she call the police? Send out a search party? Or was she overreacting? At this point, she couldn't tell. Her mind was muddled with fright.

Upon entering the stable, she immediately realized something was amiss. Several horses stomped their feet and tossed their heads when they saw her. She knew her horses' behavior as well as her own breath. Where were the friendly whickers of greeting? Why were they acting so skittish?

"Hello?" she called, hastening toward Pitonio's stall with her heart in her throat. She didn't know whether to be relieved or alarmed when Pitonio thrust his head over the top of the gate and whinnied at her.

"Hey, buddy," she said, running a soothing hand down the gelding's spotted muzzle. "I don't suppose you've seen your new friend Devon around here anywhere?"

She didn't expect an answer, so her heart leaped into next Tuesday when a low, familiar and slightly amused voice answered from deep within the shadows of the stall.

"He's closer than you think."

The cryptic answer reminded Alexis of an old scary story she used to share around the campfire. *He's three houses away. He's two houses away.*

He's closer than you think.

She probably would have been frightened half out of her wits if Griff hadn't picked that moment to reveal himself, a knowing grin on his face.

"Griff!" Alexis exclaimed, pressing her hand to her heart. "You totally frightened me."

"Sorry," he apologized; although the impish sparkle in his gray-blue eyes contradicted his words.

"No, you're not." She narrowed her gaze on him. "And for the record, I was speaking to the horse."

"I somehow doubt Pitonio here is going to provide the answers you're looking for. I, on the other hand…"

"You know where Devon is?" She brushed past his teasing to get straight to the point. "He didn't come in for supper and I was beginning to worry."

"Afraid that one of your baby chicks escaped?"

"That isn't funny, Griff." She paused and frowned as she suddenly comprehended the bizarre setting for their unusual conversation. Why were they standing on opposite sides of a stall door? "I have to ask. What are you doing in Pitonio's stall?"

"That's what I'm trying to tell you," he said with an exasperated roll of his eyes. "Devon, come say hello to Miss Grainger."

Devon hesitantly shuffled out of the shadows just as Griff had done only moments before.

What on earth?

From the red rims on his eyelids, Alexis could tell

Devon had been crying, and yet he met her with a smile.

"Devon and I were just talking," Griff explained.

"In the stable?"

Griff shrugged, as if hanging out in the back of a stall was a normal course of events for him and the boy. "I guess we lost track of time. Sorry we were late for supper. We didn't mean to worry you, did we, Devon?"

"No, sir." Devon shook his head. When he looked at Griff, his gaze was full of admiration and respect. Alexis sensed that whatever had happened between the two that afternoon, it must have been pretty major.

"No worries," she assured them.

Griff lifted a brow.

"Well, not now, anyway. I'll admit I was worried a moment ago. But it's all good, now that I know Devon was with you, safe and sound."

Griff frowned and his whole expression turned dark.

"What?" she questioned, confused by the sudden change in his countenance.

His sharp gaze captured hers. He grunted softly and gave a clipped shake of his head, warning her off the subject.

She was curious, but she followed his lead. "I set a couple of plates of food aside for you guys before I came out here. I assume you're hungry?" she asked, knowing her voice sounded abnormally bright.

"Of course we are, right, Devon?" Griff's voice didn't sound any more natural than hers. She wished she knew what issue they were dancing around—what had sent poor Devon into hiding in the stable in the first place—but she trusted Griff to let her know what was going on as soon as he could.

Apparently, Devon really was hungry, or else he was uncomfortable with the two adults together. He shot off ahead of them, back toward the ranch house. Griff started to follow, but Alexis threaded her arm through his and slowed his pace.

"Is Devon okay?" she asked softly.

Griff scoffed and shook his head. "Not even close. I don't want to violate his privacy, but he told me some things I think you ought to know about. Quite frankly, I wasn't sure how to handle what he told me."

Her grip on his arm tightened as she pulled him to a stop, turning him to face her. "That sounds ominous. Tell me what happened."

"I was rubbing Hercules down after I returned from my ride and I found Devon slumped on the ground at the back of Pitonio's stall. He'd been crying, although I doubt he'd want me to call attention to that particular fact."

"I could tell just by looking at him," Alexis acknowledged grimly. "Did he tell you why?"

"Yeah, eventually. I had to sit with him awhile before I could coax it out of him." He withdrew his arm from her grasp and wrapped it around her shoulders. "I'll tell you about it as we walk, but I'd rather not leave him to his own devices for too long right now."

The apprehension in his voice startled Alexis, sending pinpricks of shock shuddering along her nerves. "No, of course not. Let's go."

As they walked, Griff filled Alexis in on the details of his conversation with Devon. The more information Alexis received, the higher her anxiety ratcheted. The situation was far more serious and complicated than she'd anticipated. She needed time to consider what her next move should be.

By the time they reached the house, Devon was already seated at the table. The counselors had apparently had the teens clear the table before they'd left for their after-dinner activities. She'd expected to find the dishes stacked in the sink but was pleasantly surprised to discover the dishes had all been rinsed and put in the dishwasher and her kitchen was clean and shiny. It obviously hadn't taken them long to perform the task. She smiled. Her teens had learned how to work together. Hopefully that would hold them in good stead when they returned home to their regular lives.

The thought of Devon returning to his home and the situation Griff had described disturbed her, but for now she knew she needed to shelve her emotions, at least until she'd met the physical needs of the two hungry men waiting at the table.

She pulled their plates out of the refrigerator—homemade macaroni and cheese with a side of freshly creamed corn—and heated them in the microwave. She'd wrapped a plate for herself, as well, but her stomach was in knots over Devon and she wasn't sure she could swallow so much as a bite of food.

Both the man and the youth surveyed her expectantly when she sat beside them without a plate in front of her.

"You're not eating with us?" Griff queried.

"I'm not really hungry right now. I had a late lunch." Which was true, but that wasn't the real reason she didn't feel like eating. "Don't worry. I'll keep you guys company while you eat."

"Outstanding." Griff held his hand out palm up, one

arm outstretched toward Alexis and the other toward Devon. He raised his eyebrows expectantly. "Alexis, would you do the honors and lead us in prayer?"

Alexis had to fight to keep her jaw from dropping onto the floor. Hard-hearted businessman Griff Haddon suggesting prayer?

Well, knock her over with a feather.

But she wasn't about to miss the opportunity once it was presented to her. She reached for Griff's and Devon's hands and bowed her head.

"Gracious Father, thank You for giving Griff and Devon and me this special time together, just the three of us. Thank You for always watching over us and taking care of us, and for providing the food that sustains us this evening. We thank You for Your many blessings and especially for Your presence in our lives. We know You are always with us, Lord, and we are so grateful."

Two deep voices echoed her amen, and despite the dire circumstances, Alexis wanted to cheer. To see Griff and Devon taking their needs to the Father warmed her heart in a way that little else could.

Devon's face brightened, then just as quickly the smile dropped from his lips and his gaze darkened.

"What's wrong, Dev?" Alexis asked gently.

Devon's mouth twitched. "It's nothing, really. Just the way you said your prayer. It reminded me of my gran, that's all." He turned his attention to his meal, forking macaroni into his mouth with a vengeance.

Alexis met Griff's gaze and he jerked his shoulder, more of a cringe than a shrug. He was as bewildered as she was about what they could do to help poor Devon.

While the men ate, Alexis kept up a steady stream of chatter, choosing simple, frivolous subjects over trying to dive back into Devon's problems with him. She figured he was probably all talked out for the day, and anyway, he'd chosen Griff as a confidant in that regard. She didn't want to interfere in the tentative bond between them.

Devon was finished eating even before Griff was half done.

"The other teens are meeting at the boys' bunkhouse to take some first-aid training from Vee and Ben from our local fire department. Did you want to join them?" Alexis suggested, hoping the smile that accompanied her statement actually passed for a real smile. Her heart was breaking for Devon, and she knew he was trying desperately to be strong and put on a brave face to the world.

"Yeah, I'd like that, if you don't mind," he said, his gaze shifting toward Griff for permission.

"No, we don't mind at all, pal," Griff answered, affectionately slapping Devon on the back. "Go have a little fun with your friends. You don't want to spend the evening with us old fogies."

"Hey, now," Alexis protested. "Watch who you call old, here, mister. Speak for yourself, please."

Griff and Devon both chuckled, which had been her intention, then Devon turned to Alexis.

"May I please be excused?"

"Absolutely, you may. But, Devon?"

The boy was already half out of the room before she spoke. He turned at the sound of his name.

"No big deal about today, okay? All's well that ends well. But next time you want to do something different than the other teens, please check in with one of the adults so we know where to find you, okay? Promise?"

"Yes, ma'am. I promise." Devon presented her with a genuine smile and then was gone in a flash.

Alexis turned her attention to Griff. He set his fork down by his plate and steepled his fingers under his chin, a grave expression on his face.

"What are we going to do about Devon?" he asked abruptly.

Alexis's eyebrows shot up, not because he'd asked the question, but because he'd said *we,* not *you.* Despite all his protests to the contrary, he'd somehow become personally invested in the young man.

Her heart welled with appreciation. It bolstered her confidence to know she was not facing the situation alone. Griff's presence gave her strength.

"Thank you," she murmured.

This time it was his turn to look surprised. "For what?"

"For being a man Devon can look up to and confide in."

He shook his head. "I'm not so sure about the first part of the equation, but you can count on me to be there if Devon needs someone to talk to."

"I'm glad he has you."

"Don't start putting a halo on me," Griff warned, holding up his hands in protest. "I'm no saint, by any measure of the word. I just happened to be the one who was there when Devon needed a shoulder to cry on."

Alexis smiled softly. "Why do you think that is?"

Griff looked stymied. He clearly had no idea to what she was referring. He wouldn't, of course. He didn't see his own worth the way she did.

"You think it was an accident that you just *happened* to come in from your ride at the exact time when Devon needed you most? That it was all some kind of big co-incidence that you were there for him?"

He shrugged. "I guess. I don't see what else it could be."

"Well, I'll tell you what I think. I don't believe in coincidences. God had His hand in what happened this afternoon."

"God can't use me," Griff argued.

Alexis chuckled and reached her hand out to his. "He already did."

"Well, then, I don't know what He was thinking." He rubbed her palm absently with his thumb. "I don't want to be struck down by a bolt of lightning or anything for talking smack about God, but if He was working all this out, why didn't He send you or Marcus around to the stable instead of me? I don't have any training on how to deal with troubled teenagers. I was flounder-ing out there big-time, and I honestly don't know how much help I offered to the poor kid."

"I don't know why God chose to use you," Alexis admitted, although she privately had her suspicions. "But I know He did. As to why…well, you're going to have to look into your own heart for the answer to that question."

Griff cringed. "Let's not and say we did."

Alexis sensed that she'd pushed him about as far as he was able to go, spiritually speaking, at least for now. And they still had the matter of Devon to deal with.

"I have to be honest with you," she admitted. "I'm not sure what to do about Devon, or even if there is anything we *can* do."

Griff leaned forward on his elbows, his expression as determined as she'd ever seen it. He didn't release her hand. "There has to be something. We can't just look the other way and let him go back to a home where he's miserable."

"I know."

"No, you don't know." Griff slammed his free hand against the tabletop and Alexis jumped back in alarm. Griff blew out a ragged breath and combed his fingers through his hair.

"I apologize for the outburst," he said in a deceptively soft, controlled tone. "I shouldn't be taking my frustration out on you. I know you do your best for the troubled kids here at the ranch. But I saw Devon's face. The kid is hurting. You simply cannot imagine what it is like to grow up in a home without love."

Alexis was on the verge of tears, but not because he'd frightened her. She could hear the sheer agony in Griff's voice and she could not imagine the kind of horror that had put it there. Griff was a grown man, and yet here was clear evidence that what had happened to him as a child still affected him now. A strong man weakened by his past.

And she was supposed to just look away and return Devon to a similar situation?

No way. Not gonna happen. Not on her watch.

"I don't know what I can do for Devon," she reiterated sadly, but then she reached for Griff's other hand and squeezed both of them tightly. "But you can rest assured I'm going to do something, Griff."

His shoulders slumped in relief and she felt the tension leave his grasp. He really cared about what happened to Devon.

"What I was trying to say is that the issue isn't as cut and dried as it would be if, say, Devon was facing physical abuse. In that situation, I'd be able—in fact, I'd be required by law—to turn the matter over to the police. They'd make sure that Devon would have a safe place to go. But with verbal and emotional abuse it's harder to prove, and trying to bring up charges might make things harder on Devon. I think our best tactic right now is to bring in a few more people, folks who can help us wade through this mess and figure out our best course of action."

"But we will try, won't we?" His voice was agonized.

"We'll do more than try," she promised.

From her lips to God's ears.

Griff was worried about Alexis. He knew he'd been right to bring her into this situation with Devon, and not only because she was the owner of Redemption Ranch and Devon was her charge. The woman was a walking, talking example of empathy and poor Devon needed that now more than anything.

But the gift of the ability to feel what others were feeling came at a great price. What set Alexis apart and made her special was also what was causing her to appear as if she were carrying the weight of the world on her shoulders right now.

Griff knew it was because she *was* carrying the weight of the world on her shoulders—Devon's world.

Griff took a sip of hot black coffee and glanced around the table at the motley crew Alexis had assembled for this little powwow—her ragtag board of directors.

Eli and Mary were seated at Griff's right, although he didn't know if Eli was here in an official capacity as a police officer or if he was merely accompanying his wife, who was one of Alexis's best friends. Her other Little Chick friend Samantha was seated across from Griff, accompanied by her husband, Will, who was obviously ex-military. He carried himself with the fundamental strong bearing that Griff had observed to be second nature to those brave individuals who'd served the country. Last, but definitely not least, Jo Spencer was seated at the foot of the table. Griff wouldn't be surprised if she tried to take over this impromptu meeting. She was nothing if not opinionated.

Alexis was seated to Griff's left, at the head of the table, her posture stick-straight and her lips pressed into a frown. Her hands were clasped in front of her on the table, resting on top of a thick manila file folder and a legal-size yellow pad.

"Thank you all for coming on such short notice," Alexis announced, calling their spur-of-the-moment meeting to order.

"Of course, dear," Jo responded, speaking for everyone at the table. "Where else would we be? You said it was urgent. We're all here to support you, honey, in any way you need or want us to."

Alexis's bottom lip quivered and she caught it with her teeth. Griff could almost palpably feel the tension radiating from her.

He wished there was something he could do to relieve her of her burden. He wanted to wrap her in his arms and shield her from pain, to let her know how much he admired the strength of her spirit and the way that she cared about the people around her. But of course he couldn't do that. Especially not in front of everyone. He leaned as far backward as the chair would allow and crossed his arms over the width of his chest.

"BFFs to the rescue," Samantha added brightly to Jo's declaration, and both Will and Eli chuckled. Apparently they were accustomed to dropping everything to run to the assistance of one of the Little Chicks.

Griff couldn't even conceive of how it might feel to experience the kind of deep, long-standing friendship as these three women had enjoyed over the years. To think they had been friends since high school. Truly remarkable.

"Eli, I'm especially glad you could come out tonight," Alexis continued, smiling at her friend's husband. "Not in an official capacity, mind you. At least, not yet. But I need you to try to help me sort out where I stand in regard to the law."

"You did something illegal?" Mary exclaimed, and then both she and Samantha burst into giggles.

"I always knew you ladies were trouble," Eli added, elbowing his wife in the ribs with a grin full of admiration and affection.

"And yet you married one," was Jo's tongue-in-cheek response.

Griff was feeling too on edge to really appreciate the banter. In fact, it was making him kind of angry. Surely they realized they hadn't been called out here on this summer night for an evening's amusement. Maybe they didn't know any of the details yet, but why couldn't they recognize how seriously Alexis's issues were affecting her?

When he glanced at Alexis, he realized that there was reason behind the rhyme. The sparkle had returned to Alexis's electric-blue gaze, her shoulders weren't quite so tight and she was smiling gratefully at her friends.

Those friends knew exactly what they were doing—bonding with each other and pledging their support to Alexis. Her relief was evident in the lines on her face. Griff was beginning to believe there was some truth to the saying that it takes a village.

"Seriously, now," said Jo, adeptly drawing everyone's attention to the real matter at hand. "Are you in some kind of trouble, Alexis, honey? Tell us what you need us to do and consider it done."

Warmth and wonder knit together in Griff's chest and spread through his extremities like butter on toast. These people had just unconditionally committed themselves to Alexis, no questions asked. Griff had never known, never *believed,* that people like these folks existed, yet here was living proof that there was good in the world.

Alexis opened the file folder in front of her and rifled through her notes, then abruptly closed it again and gazed around the room at her friends.

"My heart is too heavy to do this in any kind of practical format. A young man's happiness, and probably his future, hangs in the balance."

"One of your teens got into trouble?" Will guessed.

"Devon's in trouble, but he didn't put himself there," Alexis responded.

"Devon," Samantha repeated. "He's the young man with the shaggy black hair, the trench coat and those big military boots, am I right?"

"Spot-on," Alexis affirmed. "I revisited his file to see what had gotten him arrested in the first place.

As it turns out, he was caught trespassing onto school grounds in the middle of the night."

"Trying to steal something?" Eli asked.

Alexis shook her head. "I don't think so. Of course, that's how it must have looked when the police came into the picture. He was caught red-handed in the science lab, using their equipment, and so of course everyone assumed he was trying to make something illegal or dangerous. But I've spoken to Devon and I don't think that's what really happened at all.

"Devon is a bright young man, but he hasn't always gotten along very well with his peers. I suspect his home life has a lot to do with that… But I'm getting ahead of myself. Some of the boys in his class were bullying him, so he regularly ditched his chemistry lab class. He broke into the school to try to complete his assignments on his own."

Eli scoffed. "And he got arrested for his efforts."

"Exactly," Alexis affirmed.

"Where were the police in all this? And his teachers? Didn't they ask him for his side of the story?" Mary sounded appalled.

"They took a formal statement from him, of course, but no one really listened to what he was saying, possibly in part because of the way he dresses. To them, he's just another punk kid getting into trouble."

Griff's gaze widened as an epiphany washed over him. That was where Alexis and her Redemption Ranch came in. She didn't judge these kids. She believed in them. No wonder she was able to make such a difference in their lives.

"He probably would have landed in jail," Alexis continued, "but because of his father's influence, he was sent to Redemption Ranch instead. His dad, Donald Parks, is a state senator and he wanted to keep his son's actions hush-hush with his constituency."

"His father didn't believe him, either?" Samantha asked. "That's terrible."

Fury knotted Griff's gut and he balled his hands into fists under the table. He wanted to punch something—or more specifically, someone. Devon's dad. But that currently wasn't an option, and it wouldn't help Alexis if he lost his cool.

"Devon's father was only thinking about himself and how Devon's actions might reflect on his own standing in society," he growled.

"But surely his mother, at least—" Samantha started, but Alexis cut her off with a jerk of the chin.

"Devon has had a really tough go of it," she explained, despondency lining her voice. "A couple of years ago, his mother was diagnosed with an especially aggressive form of cancer. She died only weeks afterward."

"Oh, my," Jo breathed. "The poor dear. I wouldn't blame him if he was acting out. Losing a mother in that fashion would be completely devastating to any teenage boy."

"It was," Alexis agreed. "And it was only made worse by his dad's reaction to his wife's passing. In his grief, he cut Devon off from all his relatives on his mother's side, most especially his beloved gran."

Alexis's friends exploded with cries of sympathy, and for a moment it was utter chaos as everyone offered their opinions one on top of the other. The poor boy, losing both his mother and grandmother. How could his father be so hard-hearted?

Griff personally thought Alexis was being way too charitable assigning the blame for Devon's father's actions on grief alone. Griff could understand anger being part of Donald Parks's grief cycle, but in Griff's opinion, it was just plain cruel to purposefully cut Devon off from contacting the one person who might have been able to give him real comfort in his time of sorrow.

"It has recently come to light that there may be even more to the story. Griff, will you share what Devon spoke to you about?"

Griff was torn. On one hand, he couldn't sit back and do nothing about Devon's situation. If these people were going to help, they needed to understand what was going on. On the other hand, he was knowingly breaking the boy's confidence. Devon trusted him. Had the young man's trust been misplaced?

Griff set his jaw. He was the adult in this relationship, and it was up to him as the mentor to recognize that the teen was in over his head and required outside aid—and even more, Griff knew he needed to do something about it. Devon had asked for his help. Pleaded, if the truth be told.

What was more, Griff truly believed all the people gathered here at this table sincerely cared about the boy's welfare. He couldn't fathom how it could be true, but he truly trusted every one of them.

Griff shared a condensed version of what had happened between him and Devon in the stable earlier that day, emphasizing the facts and glossing over the poignancy of the exchange. He knew the folks in the group would understand the emotional impact without him having to go into it.

"The question now," Alexis said when Griff had concluded, "is what I should do next. What is the best course of action under these circumstances? Devon's safety is paramount, and I definitely don't want to expose him to increased danger. Do you think I should involve the police, Eli? Or does someone have a better suggestion?"

"What happens if we bring in the cops?" Will asked.

Eli groaned and combed his fingers through the dark curls at the nape of his neck. "Police intervention might place Devon into a better situation. Then again, it could make things worse. We would have to prove there's some kind of verbal or emotional abuse happening within the home, and frankly, that's not easy to do, especially against a man as powerful as Devon's father appears to be.

"And even if we are able to make that connection, we're setting Devon up to be placed into the broken foster care system," Eli continued. "He may end up in a worse situation than where he started. It begs the question as to whether, at Devon's age, going through a questionable legal battle is even worth the effort. If he can ride it out for a couple more years, he'll be free to leave on his own, anyway."

Griff clenched his jaw until pain radiated through his head. Two years might as well be two decades for a boy in that situation. Devon was a strong young man, but frankly, Griff wasn't sure he'd last that long. But maybe there was another way—one that didn't involve police intervention.

"What about the grandmother?" Griff suggested. "Devon is very fond of her. If we can somehow inform her about what the boy is up against, maybe she'll be willing to intervene on his behalf."

"I think that's a good place to start," Alexis agreed with a relieved sigh. "It certainly can't hurt to try, although we don't have much time. Once Mission Month is over, the situation will be out of our hands."

Griff wondered if her thoughts were moving along a path similar to his. They had to do something, and if they weren't going to bring in the big guns, then they had to come up with a viable plan B, and fast.

"At this point we really know very little about the grandmother, other than what Devon has told us about her," Alexis said. "She may not know what Devon is facing at home. It's also possible that she may not be willing to step in as a guardian, or she may be unable to offer that kind of assistance for health or economic reasons."

"Devon said it was his father who forced the cut-off in the contact between them," Griff added. "She may feel she doesn't have the financial wherewithal to fight him."

"So, best case scenario, then," Alexis said, "is that the grandmother is willing and able to care for Devon, and she's not afraid to step in and stand up to his father. He's sixteen, so it wouldn't require more than a couple of years' commitment on her part before Devon will graduate from high school and be able to pursue his own ambitions."

If it was only a money issue keeping Devon and his grandmother apart, Griff had already resolved to cover their expenses, though he'd have to put a plan in place to make it an anonymous donation. He would cross that bridge when he came to it. He wanted Devon safe and happy, no matter what the cost. He considered the wisdom of sharing his thoughts with the group, but decided to keep them to himself for the time being. He'd bring it up when and if it became necessary.

"We'll hold off on making this a police matter for now," said Eli. "Certainly we can consider legal action as a viable backup plan, should the thing with the grandmother not work out for him."

"I'll contact Devon's grandmother immediately, then," Alexis affirmed, "to see if I can arrange a meeting with her as soon as possible. I'll emphasize the urgency of the matter. I believe she lives in Houston, so I can drive to see her as early as tomorrow if she's available."

"I'll accompany you," Griff offered. "We can take turns driving."

To his surprise, she reached for his hand under the cover of the table and threaded her fingers through his. He met her gaze and smiled encouragingly.

"As to the rest of us," Jo added, "we'll be your prayer warriors. Covering you all with prayer is the most effective thing we can do right now."

Griff's gaze traveled around the table. All of Alexis's friends were nodding in agreement and vocally affirming what Jo had suggested. He wasn't certain just exactly how prayer was going to help their situation, but these good folks were fervent in their belief about the Almighty's intervention, and Griff sensed his own spirit being nudged. Whether it was by God or merely the faith of those around him, he didn't know.

But it couldn't hurt to try.

"You think we ought to pray now?" he asked.

Jo beamed at him. "Why, son, that's exactly what we ought to do. Would you like to lead us?"

Panic gripped him as everyone's attention turned toward him. What had he gone and opened his big mouth for? He shook his head in fervent denial. "I'd rather not. That is… I mean…"

"I'll do it," Alexis said quickly, rescuing Griff from swallowing his own tongue. He squeezed her hand to express his gratitude, and she winked at him. "I'm the mouth of this operation," she teased with a delicate laugh that caused Griff's pulse to flare. "Griff here is the muscle."

As Griff bowed his head, he wondered if Alexis really knew just how true that statement was. He had ulterior motives for offering to accompany her on the trip to Houston to meet with Devon's grandmother. It wasn't just to set Devon's world to right, although that was certainly a large part of his motivation. But apart from that, there was Alexis. The trip was going to be hard on her. Her compassion for others laid her wide open to experiencing their pain right along with them. It was both a gift and a curse. This whole adventure would be difficult for her, and Griff wanted—*needed*—to be there to protect her in any way he could.

Muscle?

Yep, that was him, for as long as Alexis needed him. He refused to consider what would happen once they'd resolved the situation with Devon and he'd worked out the financing issues for Redemption Ranch.

Alexis wouldn't need him anymore.

The problem was he wasn't certain *he* wouldn't need *her*.

Chapter Ten

Alexis pressed her hands together in her lap and took a deep, calming breath as Griff pulled his car in front of a quaint little powder-blue cottage. It had been a mostly silent three-hour drive as they each kept to their own thoughts. Alexis tended to babble when she was nervous, but today even she couldn't think of anything inane to discuss and so she'd spent the time in prayer.

She was just glad Devon's gran had been willing to see them on such quick notice. It was the Monday of the last week of Devon's stay at the ranch and they had very little time to resolve his issues.

Rosebushes with a variety of pink and red blooms lined the walkway and the front of the house. Pretty baskets with an assortment of vivid annuals hung on either side of the doorway. The yard was green and trimmed and well-kept. The whole place looked bright and welcoming.

"This is it," Griff confirmed, shutting off his GPS. He laid his large, warm hands over both of hers. "Take a deep breath and try to relax."

"I've been taking so many deep breaths I'm feeling

light-headed. You don't happen to have a paper bag on you in case I hyperventilate, do you?"

He chuckled. "The house looks promising, don't you think?"

Alexis laughed dryly. "You mean it's unlikely that an old hag would keep such a nice yard?"

One corner of his lips rose. "Something like that."

Alexis hiccupped, holding in an unexpected sob. "I just feel bad that we have to spring something so dark and awful on some nice little old lady. She sounded so shocked when I called."

"Yes, but she agreed to meet with us."

"Oh, definitely. She was delighted that I'd phoned her. One thing I'm already completely convinced of is that she loves her grandson to pieces and misses his presence in her life."

"Then this ought to be fairly straightforward. We inform her of the circumstances surrounding Devon and his father and find out what, if anything, she wants to do or can do for him, right?"

"Right." She blew out a breath. "Let's go before I lose my nerve." Alexis steeled herself to stay calm. A boy's happiness rode on the outcome of today's meeting.

Griff exited the car and came around to open the door for her. He was nothing if not a gentleman. She smiled her thanks, but she didn't anticipate him stopping her when she tried to move past him.

His hand snaked out around her waist and before she could anticipate what he was doing, he brushed a soft, sweet kiss against her cheek.

Her heart thudded rapidly as she pressed her palm over the spot his lips had touched. "What was that for?"

His gray-blue eyes twinkled. "I just wanted you to know that no matter what happens in there, you're not alone. Okay?"

Unable to form words, she nodded. As well-meaning and innocent as he might have meant the gesture to be, his action had her pulse racing and her mind spinning—at exactly the time when she most needed to have her head on straight. Yet it felt just *right,* somehow, when he reached for her hand.

They were facing this trial together. She'd never been more thankful than she was at this moment that her ditzy twin sister had concocted the outrageous matchmaking scheme that had brought Griff into her life.

Her courage and her hope soared as she rang the doorbell. A moment later a tiny white-haired woman answered the door. She leaned heavily against a cane and was hunched over with age, yet her gaze was clear and intelligent. Alexis now knew where Devon got his striking brown eyes.

"You must be Alexis and Griff. Please, come in. I've got coffee brewing." Devon's gran led them through a simple, country-decorated living space and into a small kitchen, where she'd set up coffee service. A yellow Bundt cake dusted with powdered sugar graced the middle of the table. Despite the knots in her stomach, the rich smell of the baked good had Alexis's mouth watering.

"Thank you so much for seeing us today, Mrs. Corbin," Alexis said, allowing Griff to usher her to a seat at the table. He waited to seat himself until after he'd offered the same kindness to the old woman.

"Please, call me Hannah," the woman replied.

"Pleased to meet you, Hannah," Griff said as he helped her scoot her chair in to the table.

"I'm so glad you both have come. You have news about my Devon?"

"We do," Alexis affirmed. Her heart was pounding in her ears. "I'm afraid it's not all good."

"Oh, dear." Hannah reached for the knife to cut the cake, but Griff gently took it from her grasp. "I was afraid of that. You sounded rather serious when you called me."

"Allow me," Griff said, cutting neat slices of the cake for her and serving both of the ladies present.

"Thank you, dear."

"As you may or may not know," Alexis said, "Devon was sent to my ranch—Redemption Ranch is the name of it—to avoid community service for a crime he was accused of committing."

"Crime, my eye," Hannah retorted with a scoff. "I don't know what you think he did, but I'm telling you right now that my grandson isn't capable of committing a crime. He's got a heart of gold, that one, and it isn't my bias as his gran making me say it."

"We agree with you," Alexis assured her. "While he did admit to breaking into his school, he did so with honorable intentions, and we believe he was mistakenly convicted. However, God works in mysterious ways. I'm grateful he was sent into my care at the ranch. It has been a true joy getting to know him. He's a very special young man. I see a lot of potential in him."

"Alexis has really helped him come out of his shell," Griff added. "She does an amazing job with the teenagers. She even refers to them as her kids."

Alexis flashed Griff a grateful smile.

"While at the ranch, we've become aware of some information regarding Devon's home life that we've found...troubling," she continued.

Hannah had her cup of coffee nearly to her lips, but she set it back down again. "Tell me."

Alexis was a little worried that sharing her fears about Devon would be too much for the old woman to bear, but when she met Hannah's determined gaze, she knew the woman was much stronger than her frail body suggested.

"Devon has admitted to us that he is not comfortable going back home to live with his father," Griff inserted. "We don't believe the man has been physically abusive—yet. But we have reason to suspect that at the very least, Devon has been emotionally neglected. We believe it may not be in his best interests to return home."

"No," Hannah agreed, her voice cracking with strain. "No, I should say not. Donald has never been an easy man to live with, but at least when my daughter was alive, Devon was well cared for and greatly loved."

"Devon loved his mother very much, as well," Alexis assured her.

"Yes, well, after her death, Donald barred me from seeing my grandson. It broke my heart, but I accepted his conditions because I thought if I did, Donald would go easier on Devon. I see now that I was wrong in that assumption. I should have fought him back then. I *will* fight him now."

Alexis was awash in relief. Having a relative in their corner would be far preferable to bringing in the law and throwing Devon—who was already so skittish and reluctant to trust—into the broken foster care system.

"If I had known things had gotten this bad— Oh, why didn't I trust my instincts? I should have been there for him," Hannah said, ending on a sob.

"We're not here to cast blame," Alexis assured her, gently patting her shoulder. "You couldn't have known how bad things would become. No one knew."

"But we're sure appreciative of your willingness to help us out now, ma'am," Griff added. "Help Devon, that is."

"Just tell me what you think we should do." Her wrinkled cheeks were wet with tears but her eyes were glowing with renewed determination.

"I'll be honest with you," Alexis said, sliding her hand to Hannah's forearm. "I've been doing some research. As you know, Donald is a very powerful man with a lot of money to sling around."

"I've got money, too," Griff growled. "As much as you need to fight this. Don't let that hinder you."

"Yes, well, that's the point," Alexis countered. "We've already come to the conclusion that fighting it through a legal battle should be our last resort. We believe it would be better for us and for Devon if we can come up with a way to confront Donald directly."

"It's me that should do the confronting," Hannah affirmed. "I've got a lot to say to Donald, things I've kept to myself for far too long."

"You don't want to get him riled," Griff cautioned, holding up his hands, "or he might not listen to reason."

Hannah snorted. "Donald has never been one to listen to reason. But I'm going to give it my best shot."

"Would you like us to come with you?" Alexis offered. "We would be more than happy to, Hannah."

Frankly, Alexis was more than a little worried about

what a confrontation between Hannah and Donald might look like. She would never forgive herself if she accidentally placed Hannah in danger; never mind what might happen to Devon if this all went south.

"No," Hannah retorted sharply. "This is between me and him. I've got your number. I'll call you as soon as I know anything. In the meantime, keep me in prayer."

"I have a whole team praying for this endeavor." And now she was especially glad of it—and that Devon's grandmother was a praying woman. She would be glad to see the boy make a new home with her. He and his gran would be so happy together.

Please, Lord, let it be so.

Griff was out in the chicken coop watching the teenagers gathering eggs. Two days had gone by in relative peace. They'd heard from Hannah that she'd planned to meet with Donald yesterday, but she'd never called back to let them know what the outcome had been.

Griff found himself keeping a running conversation with God going in his head. He didn't know when his relationship with the Almighty had become personal. It wasn't like a bolt of lightning or a sudden emotional conversion. It was more that he'd just slowly become aware of God's presence in his life and was now choosing to acknowledge it. He even thought he might attend church with Alexis on Sunday.

He thought church might be a good place to be able to pass his thanks—secretly, of course—on to the many members of the community who had already committed to backing Redemption Ranch. Alexis had more friends than she probably realized, and he was not the least bit surprised that they all recognized what an important contribution she made to the community. Her financing for Redemption Ranch was coming together without a hitch.

He was more worried about what was happening between Hannah and Donald. He would at least have expected her to call, even if things hadn't gone as well as she had hoped they would. She knew they were waiting to hear about it. Either way, he and Alexis needed to know what Devon was about to face.

He'd just picked up a bag of feed for the kids to spread for the chickens when he heard a commotion coming from the front of the house. It sounded like a man's voice, and he was yelling. Alexis was by herself, cooking supper. Griff dropped the sack of feed into the dirt and took off at a dead run.

He skidded to a stop after he turned the corner to the front of the house. There was a black SUV in the driveway that Griff didn't recognize. A middle-aged, dark-haired man stood on the front porch with Hannah, his keys clenched in one hand and Hannah's collar clenched in the other. The poor old woman didn't have her cane to steady her and he had her dangling half off her feet. It appeared that the man, whom Griff assumed to be Donald Parks, had dragged her up to the porch.

"Get your hands off her," Griff demanded, bolting into action. He ran up the porch steps and faced Donald off, meeting his gaze squarely and with a glare that he knew communicated the disgust he felt in his heart about this man.

He heard the door open behind him. "What's going on here?" Alexis challenged, stepping up beside Griff. "How dare you manhandle your mother-in-law. Let her go this instant."

"She's not my mother-in-law anymore," Donald growled. "And I'm not here about her. Now, I demand to see my son."

"You are on private property, sir, and you have no right to demand anything," Alexis informed him in a deceptively calm voice. Griff could see by the flush on her cheeks that she was barely reining in her temper. "I won't repeat myself again. Let. Go. Of. Hannah."

Donald shoved the old woman forward and she cried out in surprise and pain. Griff barely caught her before she fell.

"It's okay, Hannah," he quietly assured her as he led her to the porch swing and helped her sit.

"No, it's not. It's not okay." Hannah sounded hysterical. "He's not listening to reason at all. He practically kidnapped me when he brought me down here."

"Hannah, you're overreacting," Donald barked. "You started this. And I did no such thing."

"Taking me somewhere against my will is kidnapping, Donald Parks, no matter what you call it," Hannah argued hotly.

"I refuse to argue about this." Donald turned to Alexis and stepped well into her personal space.

Griff didn't like the way Donald tried to use his superior height to intimidate her. Alexis was a tall woman, but Donald still had a good six inches on her and was a hundred pounds heavier. He was using his size to his advantage, pressing in on her, hovering over her.

Griff growled and stepped between them.

"Lay off, Parks," he demanded.

"I'm not leaving until I have my son. I want to see Devon. Bring him to me. Right now."

"No." Griff wasn't about to let Devon anywhere near this raving lunatic, at least until the man had calmed down, and probably not even then.

"I am that boy's father and his legal guardian. You have no right to keep me away from him."

"Maybe not," Alexis replied, slipping under Griff's shoulder and wrapping her arm around his waist. "But you listen to me, and you listen well. I'm this close to calling the police." She held up her hand, marking the distance of about an inch with her thumb and forefinger. "I may not have the right to stop you, but they do. You won't be seeing Devon anytime soon if you're behind bars."

"Under what charges?" he bellowed. "You can't have me arrested. I haven't done anything wrong."

Alexis lifted a brow, the same way she did when the teenagers were giving her problems. To Griff's surprise, the expression worked essentially the same way with Donald. He'd been about to say more, but when Alexis narrowed her gaze on him, he closed his mouth and took an involuntary step backward.

"I can tick off a dozen different reasons the cops can put you in jail," she said in a threatening tone, but it wasn't a threat. It was the truth.

There was not only the potential of the verbal and emotional abuse he'd heaped on Devon, which was in itself likely worse even than Griff had imagined, now that he'd seen Donald in person. He knew all about men like Donald, with their all-or-nothing tempers. No wonder Devon was miserable.

But now Donald had added his treatment of Hannah to the mix. Even if the police didn't immediately believe Devon's testimony, they would most certainly listen to Hannah's. Especially if the policeman in question happened to be Eli, who was on their side already. And then there was the fact that Donald had barged onto private property and was verbally threatening all of those present.

"I'll take you down," he snarled. "Your Redemption Ranch will be nothing after I get through with it."

Alexis scoffed. "Feel free to try. There won't be anything left for you to take, anyway. Your threats mean nothing to me."

Griff had to swallow his outrage. Alexis really believed what she'd just said. She thought her ministry was at an end. He wanted to speak up, to assure her that her entire world wasn't crumbling down around her. But maybe it was just as well that she didn't yet know. In her current state, she wouldn't be cowed by Donald's threats.

"You don't know who you're speaking with," Donald snapped. "I'm a state senator. I have powerful allies."

"Not in this town, you don't," Alexis countered swiftly. "Keep in mind these are local police, folks I grew up with. You think they're going to believe you, or me? If I ask them nicely, you may not even get a single phone call from jail."

Donald's eyes glazed over in rage and he shrieked in frustration, sending a chill down Griff's spine. The guy was diving off the cliff of sanity and right into the raging river of crazy.

Every muscle in Griff's body wound into a tight knot as he prepared to spring into instant action. He could fight if he had to, and he wouldn't wait until Donald had injured one of the women in his care before he acted. He wouldn't hesitate to throw the first punch if the situation escalated any further.

Donald's gaze met Griff's and for a moment the challenge was evident, but then the light left his eyes and he sagged backward. Griff didn't trust the movement and stepped forward, effectively blocking him from the two women.

Donald held his hands up in defeat. "All right, all right. You win."

"I suggest you sit and calm down," Alexis inserted, laying her hand on Griff's shoulder.

Donald slumped down on the porch stairs and ran a hand across his face. He looked tired and defeated, as if all the energy had left his body.

"I just want to see my son," he reiterated, this time in a calmer tone.

"Don't you believe that," Hannah warned. "He doesn't want to see Devon, he wants to take him away from the ranch."

Donald glared at Hannah. "As is my right."

Griff sighed inwardly. It sounded as if they were back to square one.

"I will speak to you about Devon, but I am not prepared to bring him into your presence at this time," Alexis informed him.

"What's to talk about? I'm his dad and I'm here to take him home."

"See? I tried to reason with him," Hannah said. "All he did was get angry and drag me out here without explaining where we were going or what he was doing."

"I fail to see why it's anyone's business but mine what I do with my son," Donald barked.

"It's your son's business," Alexis replied. "And it

became ours when he indicated his disinclination to return to your home."

"He *what?*" Donald roared.

Griff stepped forward, but Alexis held him back. "This is your last warning, Mr. Parks. If you raise your voice again, I will call the police."

Donald snapped his jaw shut and scowled.

"We have reason to believe Devon has experienced verbal and emotional abuse in your home, and your attitude right now is only confirming what we suspect to be true," Alexis informed him, her tone incredibly calm and reasonable under the circumstances. Griff was impressed with her decorum.

Donald started to stand, but Griff grabbed his shoulder and pushed him back down again.

"Keep your seat," Griff warned.

"You have no proof," Donald informed them coldly. "Abuse is a heavy word with which to threaten me. I suggest you think carefully before you start spouting off unsupported nonsense."

"No," Griff retorted. "I suggest you think very carefully about what your next words are going to be. We've documented enough to make a pretty airtight case against you."

Griff was grasping for straws, but he wasn't about to let Donald know that. He figured there was probably a lot more he didn't know about Donald's treatment of Devon, and he was banking on the fact that Donald *would* be taking all that into consideration.

It worked. Donald blanched. "Are you suggesting you're planning to press charges against me? You'll never get away with it. I'll be exonerated."

"Perhaps. Perhaps not," Alexis said, moving once

again to Griff's side. "The way I see it, you're going to lose either way, because you can depend on the fact that if you force this issue, I'm going to make this trial go so public your head will spin. I will call every local and national news agency I can get a number for. Even if you're eventually cleared of the charges, people will associate your name with child abuse. Your career will be ruined. I'll make absolutely sure of that."

Harsh, but exactly what Donald needed to hear. Alexis was a brave woman. Griff admired her now more than ever.

"However, providing you agree to my terms, I see no need to bring the police in on this matter when there is an amicable solution right in front of us."

Donald's eyes clouded in confusion. Then he glanced over his shoulder and nodded in understanding. "You're talking about Hannah."

"Yes," Alexis confirmed. "Hannah."

"I'm listening."

"I propose that Devon live with his grandmother until he reaches the age of majority. He has already agreed this would be in his best interest and is excited to make a home with Hannah, as she is with him."

"He would be," Donald mumbled, and then straightened his shoulders. "But he is my son."

"Which is, of course, why you'll see that this is truly the best thing for him." Alexis paused and coughed into her fist. "And for you."

"And if I agree?"

"You'll make it legal. Those are my terms. Hannah will become Devon's legal guardian until he reaches the age of majority. Assuming she concurs, she may allow you to visit them when it's convenient with Devon's school schedule to do so, but that is providing you do so on her terms and with her rules."

"I'm the rule-maker here," Donald insisted.

"In that case, I'm afraid our offer will not be possible." Alexis pulled her cell phone from the back pocket of her jeans and offhandedly waved it in his direction. "You agree to our terms, or no deal. There's no room for compromise here. I'm quite prepared to phone the police. It's your call."

The silence was deafening. There was not even an insect or animal that dared to break the sudden quiet. Griff wasn't breathing, and from the expressions on Alexis's and Hannah's faces, he guessed they weren't, either.

"I accept."

"What was that?" Griff demanded.

"I said I accept. I'll have the papers drawn up and delivered to Hannah. She can keep the brat."

Griff couldn't believe his ears.

Just like that, it was over and Donald was gone, leaving Hannah behind to rejoice with her grandson.

It was a happy moment for Griff, but a bittersweet one, as well. Devon was safe. Redemption Ranch was safe.

The only thing that wasn't safe was Griff's heart.

Chapter Eleven

The rest of the week went quickly for Alexis. She'd made up the guest bedroom for Hannah, who'd decided to stay at the ranch while the legal proceedings were under way. Surprisingly true to his word, Donald Park had had the papers delivered within a couple of days. Devon would truly be going home with his grandmother, and Alexis could not be more pleased and grateful. In fact, Hannah and Devon were staying through the weekend. Hannah had expressed an interest in attending one of their church services at the chapel, and Alexis knew that everyone involved in bringing the plan to fruition would want to rejoice with them.

But as she said goodbye to the rest of the teens on Friday, her mood had gone from emotional to just plain gloomy. It was hard for her to believe it was over. Redemption Ranch would be closing its doors. She had no idea where to go from here. What would she do for a living? Where would she even live? The bank would foreclose once it became clear that she couldn't keep up with her mortgage payments.

She was still pondering her future when she walked into the chapel on Sunday morning with Hannah and Devon at her side. She was in desperate need of God's comfort. She put on the best face that she could for their sakes, knowing they were there to rejoice over God's many blessings in their lives. She didn't want to ruin it for them.

To her surprise, she found Griff standing in the vestibule to the chapel. He was dressed in a gray suit that Alexis guessed would cost a cowboy a month's salary. He'd shaved and his hair was carefully groomed. He looked relieved when he spotted her, and with the smile he greeted her with, Alexis thought she'd never seen such a handsome man in her life.

But it wasn't just his good looks that sent her heart into overdrive. She loved everything about Griff Haddon. Somewhere in the past month, he'd become her right-hand man, the person she turned to with both her troubles and her blessings.

What was she going to do without him? He'd spent the week looking at various potential properties, and she'd seen him several times with Jo Spencer, their heads together as they whispered in conspiratorial tones. He was leaving, and there wasn't a thing she could do about it.

Not *leaving* leaving, of course. He was staying in Serendipity. They'd be neighbors. But their relationship would change, and she didn't like change. Her whole world was going up in ashes and she was powerless to stop it.

"You look tired," Griff said as he approached.

"Why, thank you." She hoped her response didn't

sound as snappy as she felt. She didn't know how much restraint she had left.

He laid a hand on the small of her back. "I didn't mean that as an insult. I'm just concerned. You've been burning the candle at both ends between this deal with Devon and making sure the rest of the kids got home okay."

"Well, it's over, isn't it?" This time she knew she sounded short with him.

He pressed his lips together. "I'm sorry, babe," he whispered.

Why was he treating her so kindly? She didn't deserve it, not with the mood she was in. She wasn't good for company right now. Maybe church had been a mistake. She shouldn't be around people right now and she was in no state of mind to rejoice in the Lord. If it wasn't for Devon and Hannah, she would turn right around and go home, get back into bed, cover up her head and stay there.

"There's Jo," Griff said, nodding toward the red-haired woman who was boisterously making her rounds around the room greeting everyone she met. "If you'll excuse me a minute, I need to go speak with her. Will you save me a seat in the sanctuary?"

She nodded and he started to walk away, but she caught the sleeve of his jacket. "I forgot to ask, what are you doing here?" She stopped and shook her head, disgusted with herself. "That sounded really bad. Of course you're welcome in church. I was just surprised to see you here."

"Not as surprised as I am to be here." He grinned widely. "But to answer your question, I'm here for the same reason everyone else is. To get to know God better."

"Really?" Her heart flooded with warmth, especially when he winked at her.

"Really. Now I'd better catch Jo before I lose her."

As she watched him walk away, she marveled at the changes in him. He wasn't the same man who'd raided her kitchen on that first morning. He'd always carried himself with a masculine kind of confidence, but now he seemed to have an added poise. He spoke to everyone he passed as if they were friends—and they were. He'd found a real home here in Serendipity.

She was happy for him. She really was. But it was hard for her to see the good when her own life was in such shambles. She had to buck up and face reality. A handsome guy such as Griff would find a nice girl here in town and settle down for real. Meanwhile, she'd have to find a job, and jobs were scarce in Serendipity. She was even toying with joining Vivian in Houston, though that prospect brought her down more than anything.

She didn't really feel like talking to anybody, so she made her way into the sanctuary and found a seat in her usual pew. With a sigh, she knelt, closed her eyes and clasped her hands. She desperately needed the peace that only God could give.

She felt rather than saw Griff sit next to her in the pew. She didn't know how she knew it was Griff. Maybe it was the spicy scent of the aftershave he always wore, but she thought it might simply be that she was used to him there, next to her. When he knelt beside her and slipped his arm around her waist, she knew for sure it was him. And she knew for sure how hard it was going to be to let him go.

"It's okay, honey," he whispered in her ear. "You know when God closes a window, he opens a door."

"I think you've got it backward," she whispered back, but his statement made her chuckle despite her bleak mood.

"Whatever. I'm right, though, aren't I? God's got this?"

God's got this.

Griff's words echoed over and over again in her mind as the service started. How could a man so new to his faith have hit the nail so completely on the head? It made her question her own lack of faith.

She had nothing. Did that mean God had something completely different in mind for her, some new adventure for her to follow? She had to believe He did.

She prayed through the whole service, seeking God's guidance on her future. She didn't expect a bolt of lightning or anything, but she was grateful to feel the Lord's presence and His peace as she sought His face. By the time Pastor Shawn gave the benediction, Alexis was in a better place. She didn't know what would happen or where she would be, but she knew Who would be with her.

Alexis was putting her hymnal away after the final hymn when Pastor Shawn stopped everyone by announcing he had something special to say. He held up his hands until everyone quieted and settled themselves in the pews.

"I'd appreciate it if I can have everyone's attention for just a moment. There's someone here today who has got a special announcement to make."

Alexis was shocked when Griff stood to his feet and moved up to the front of the sanctuary.

"I appreciate you all hanging out here for a second," Griff said, easily taking over the role of orator from Pastor Shawn. "As you know, I'm a relative newcomer to Serendipity and a brand-spanking newcomer to this church."

He waited while people clapped and shouted in welcome.

"I do appreciate you all, more than I can say. Not only have you welcomed me to town, but you've helped me establish myself here. You've given me plenty of good leads on land I can call my own, and you've held out the hand of friendship to me.

"But it's not for me that I'm up here today. I'm here about a very worthy cause that you all know about. Alexis, if you would join me up here?"

Alexis's heart jammed into her throat. What was going on here? Why was Griff asking for her, of all people? And what was the worthy cause he'd mentioned?

She stood and stumbled up the aisle. With everyone's eyes on her, it was reminiscent of a wedding. She hoped she wouldn't be this klutzy on that occasion, should it ever happen.

When her gaze met and locked with Griff's, the odd premonition of being a bride only increased. His eyes were full of male admiration and his smile left no doubt how much he appreciated her. She could only smile back, even as she realized that her life was more of a mess than ever. She was looking into the eyes of the man she was in love with. A man who was standing up there looking every bit the handsome groom, but who no doubt did not return her feelings.

And the entire town was looking on. How awkward could this be? She wanted to turn around and run right out of the sanctuary, but she was committed, so she did the only thing she could.

She kept walking. Right up to the front of the aisle. Right up to his side. Pastor Shawn was standing between them, his Bible tucked in his hands.

Alexis was blushing to the roots of her hair. Did anyone else in this room see the incredibly awkward parallels going on here?

She sucked in a deep breath. They probably did. It was hard to miss. And although it felt incredibly painful to her now, she reminded herself that this was definitely the kind of situation she would be able to laugh at later. She'd probably be telling this to her grandchildren forty years from now.

If she had grandchildren...

The thought made her sad, because she couldn't imagine her family without the man standing beside her being a part of it. When had her life become such a crazy mess?

Griff reached for her hand and turned her to face him. Yet another similarity to a wedding ceremony. She squeezed her eyes shut for a moment and then mentally shrugged. She had to snap out of it or she was never going to get through this.

Whatever *this* was.

"Redemption Ranch," Griff said, smiling down at her, "has been an important part of the community for several years now."

The ranch. This was about the ranch. Her gaze darted to his but he didn't give anything away in his eyes.

"But as you all know, Alexis and her ranch have not only contributed to the good of Serendipity, but to the lives of dozens of troubled teenagers. To say her ministry is worthwhile is a blatant understatement. It's important. No—it's crucial."

Tears sprang to Alexis's eyes at the nods and murmurs that went around the congregation. She'd never felt so much love as she did at that moment.

"That is why I'm happy to be standing up here today to announce to Alexis and this community that Redemption Ranch will be continuing its good work well into the foreseeable future. Many, many teenagers will thank you for your effort, Alexis."

As the congregation began clapping, Alexis looked up at Griff in confusion. "I—I don't understand."

He tapped the end of her nose with his finger. "Did you think I was going to help your sister achieve her dreams and watch yours flounder to a halt? I don't think so. You've got your ministry sponsors. Redemption Ranch is a go."

Tears streamed unheeded down Alexis's face but she didn't bother wiping them away as she launched herself into Griff's arms. "Thank you. Thank you. Thank you," she repeated, squeezing him tightly around the neck.

He laughed and swung her around, then set her back on her feet again. "I appreciate the gratitude, honey, but you're thanking the wrong person." He made a grand gesture, sweeping his hand around to indicate the people in the congregation. "These are the folks who deserve the real thanks."

"What?" Her head was spinning and her heart was so full of joy that she wasn't quite sure she was following what he was saying.

"It's simple. Meet your new ministry partners."

"My new…ministry partners," she repeated, feeling entirely bemused. Her friends and neighbors were the ones who'd committed to preserving Redemption Ranch? "But they have obligations. Families to feed. They can't—"

"We can and we did," Jo announced from the front row where she always sat. "And not a word out of you, missy. The Lord says we are to be generous with all the blessings He's given us. And that's exactly what we're doing. We're believin' and we're givin'."

"I…" Alexis stopped, too choked up to speak. "Thank you doesn't seem like enough. There are no words."

"Thank you is plenty enough words," Jo assured her, and the congregation once again burst into applause. Even Hannah and Devon wholeheartedly joined in with the whoops and hollers.

"So there you have it," said Griff, squeezing her waist. "You can arrange for your next group of trouble."

"I'll do that."

"Oh, and one other thing," he said, as if it was an afterthought.

"What's that?"

He flashed her a cheeky grin. "You can hire that administrative-assistant-slash-accountant that you so desperately need."

His gaze caught hers and she saw something there that she hadn't seen before. He seemed to be asking something. His gorgeous gray-blue eyes were pleading with her for—

What?

"I was rather hoping I could hire you," she said, feeling suddenly shy, especially since they were still in full view of a curious audience.

"I was hoping you'd say that," he said, sounding relieved. "But am I pushing it if I say I was wishing for a little more than a job offer? I kind of still need a place to live and I was thinking that maybe…well…"

He dropped to one knee and Alexis's heart stopped dead in her chest. Suddenly she knew what it was she'd been reading in Griff's gaze, even before he pulled a small velvet box from the pocket of his jacket.

Was this…? How could this be happening to her? An hour ago her life was as low as it had ever been. She'd thought every door and window had been slammed in her face.

And now?

Now she was looking at her future, and it was full of life in every conceivable way.

Her ranch. Her teenagers.

Griff.

"You're killing me down here," he said with a shaky laugh. "Are you going to answer my question?"

Her face heated until she knew she must be a bright red. She'd gotten so flustered she hadn't heard a question.

"I'm sorry, I—"

Griff swallowed hard, the smile dropping from his lips. "Please don't say no, Alexis. If you need to wait, I understand, but—"

She cut him off with a kiss before he could say another word. "I'm not saying no," she assured him between kisses. "I seriously didn't hear the question. I'm slow, but I think I can figure it out from here."

"Oh, man, you had me worried there for a second," he said through a ragged breath.

She dragged him to his feet. "Yes, yes, I'll marry you. Oh, my goodness. I can't believe I could feel so happy. An hour ago I thought…well…forget what I thought an hour ago. Yes. Yes!"

Griff laughed, slid the diamond on her finger and kissed her hard, and the congregation exploded, echoing the joy Alexis was feeling in her heart.

"Did anyone else kind of feel the whole wedding vibe here?" Samantha asked, rushing up the aisle to be the first to congratulate her friend. "Like Griff standing at the front of the aisle, and her walking up to him? Pastor Shawn officiating?"

"I thought so, too," agreed Mary, who was right on her heel.

"So everyone will come back for the real thing, right?" Griff asked, wagging his eyebrows.

"You'd better believe it." As usual, Jo Spencer answered for the whole crowd.

"There's no rush, but I'd like to speak to you folks about supporting the ministry of Redemption Ranch," Hannah added, embracing them both. "You've done so very much for my Devon. I'd consider it an honor to help other teenagers in his position."

In moment they were surrounded by people. Their friends. Their neighbors. Their ministry partners.

Griff pulled her close as they accepted the well-wishes of the community they both loved. When the crowd finally started thinning, he pulled her around to face him.

"I know you missed the part where I asked you to be my wife," he said with a chuckle, "so I wanted to reiterate that you're going to marry me, right?"

"I want that in writing," she insisted.

"Oh, you can count on that, honey," he replied, brushing a kiss across her cheek. "I'm ready to sign, seal and deliver on that wedding license. The sooner, the better, as far as I'm concerned. But since you didn't hear my proposal, you might have missed another important fact I mentioned to you."

"Yeah?" she asked, gazing up at him with so much joy in her heart that she thought she might burst from the feel of it. "And what's that?"

"I love you," he murmured. "I can't even believe how much I love you. I never knew this much love even existed in the world, until I met you."

Alexis stopped breathing and perhaps the world stopped turning. "I love you, too, Griff. Now and forever."

"Did I mention I'd like to have a lot of kids?" He grinned impishly and his eyebrows danced.

She burst into laughter. "Oh, you're going to get them, all right. A whole new crop at the beginning of each of our new Mission Months."

"Hmm," he said, narrowing his teasing gaze on her. "Not that I mind loads and loads of troubled teenagers, mind you. But I meant *our* kids. Yours and mine. Together."

She cupped his face in her hands and pulled his head down until his lips hovered just over hers. "Those, too, my love. Those, too."

* * * * *

Dear Reader,

Welcome to the final book in my Serendipity Sweetheart series. With Alexis and Griff's story, all three of Serendipity's Little Chicks have finally found their happily-ever-afters.

Have you ever experienced a time in your life when you believed a specific situation, person or thing was what you needed, only to discover the exact opposite was true? Griff Haddon thought he was looking for solitude and anonymity in Serendipity, when the real desire of his heart was to be loved and accepted into family and community. He didn't realize God's blessings would be so much bigger than he could have imagined.

God loves you fiercely and furiously. He has a plan for your life that is lovely beyond what you can imagine. He knows even when you do not what will bring you the most joy and happiness in your life, and I pray you'll experience all of the fullness of joy His love can bring.

I hope you enjoyed *Redeeming the Rancher*. I love to connect with you, my readers, in a personal way. Please look me up at www.debkastnerbooks.com. I'm on Facebook at www.facebook.com/debkastnerbooks, or you can catch me on Twitter @debkastner.

Please know that you are daily in my prayers.

Love Courageously,

Deb Kastner

Questions for Discussion

1. At the beginning of the novel, Griff has been hurt by a woman and consequently believes all women are not to be trusted. Have you ever been hurt by someone and struggled not to make generalizations based on your experience?

2. Why does Griff want to raise horses? Do you think he truly understands his reasons at the beginning of the story?

3. Alexis tends to put off thinking about her problems, rather than dwelling on them. Is this healthy? How do you address the anxieties in your life?

4. Why do you think Griff bonded with Devon?

5. Alexis has a cup-half-full—even when it's tipped over!—outlook on life. Griff sees the bad before the good. Which character is more like you?

6. Why did Vivian really send Griff to Serendipity? As a lark or for her own selfish gain? Can/Did God use her actions for good despite her mistakes?

7. With which character did you most relate? Why?

8. Vivian loves celebrating her birthday, whereas Alexis would rather avoid it. Which camp do you fall in and why?

9. Jo Spencer is affectionately known as the town's second mother. Do you have someone in your life that supports you spiritually and emotionally?

10. What are the major themes of this novel? What is the take-away value for your life?

11. Griff had never experienced small-town living before. How is Serendipity different from a larger town?

12. At the beginning of the novel, Griff comes into Serendipity looking for solitude and anonymity. What does he find instead?

13. Serendipity has a strong sense of community. There are many types of communities. Name some communities you are involved in.

14. At the end of the novel, Alexis tells Griff that God worked through him to solve Devon's problem—and hers. Why do you think Griff had a hard time believing this could be so?

15. Mother Teresa is quoted as saying, "If you can't feed a hundred people, feed just one." Alexis lived her life this way in serving the troubled teens. Who in your life can you feed with God's love?

REQUEST YOUR FREE BOOKS!

2 FREE INSPIRATIONAL NOVELS
PLUS 2
FREE
MYSTERY GIFTS

Love Inspired

YES! Please send me 2 FREE Love Inspired® novels and my 2 FREE mystery gifts (gifts are worth about $10). After receiving them, if I don't wish to receive any more books, I can return the shipping statement marked "cancel." If I don't cancel, I will receive 6 brand-new novels every month and be billed just $4.74 per book in the U.S. or $5.24 per book in Canada. That's a saving of at least 21% off the cover price. It's quite a bargain! Shipping and handling is just 50¢ per book in the U.S. and 75¢ per book in Canada.* I understand that accepting the 2 free books and gifts places me under no obligation to buy anything. I can always return a shipment and cancel at any time. Even if I never buy another book, the two free books and gifts are mine to keep forever.

105/305 IDN F47Y

Name _____ (PLEASE PRINT) _____

Address _____ Apt. # _____

City _____ State/Prov. _____ Zip/Postal Code _____

Signature (if under 18, a parent or guardian must sign) _____

Mail to the Harlequin® Reader Service:
IN U.S.A.: P.O. Box 1867, Buffalo, NY 14240-1867
IN CANADA: P.O. Box 609, Fort Erie, Ontario L2A 5X3

**Are you a subscriber to Love Inspired books
and want to receive the larger-print edition?
Call 1-800-873-8635 or visit www.ReaderService.com.**

* Terms and prices subject to change without notice. Prices do not include applicable taxes. Sales tax applicable in N.Y. Canadian residents will be charged applicable taxes. Offer not valid in Quebec. This offer is limited to one order per household. Not valid for current subscribers to Love Inspired books. All orders subject to credit approval. Credit or debit balances in a customer's account(s) may be offset by any other outstanding balance owed by or to the customer. Please allow 4 to 6 weeks for delivery. Offer available while quantities last.

Your Privacy—The Harlequin® Reader Service is committed to protecting your privacy. Our Privacy Policy is available online at www.ReaderService.com or upon request from the Harlequin Reader Service.

We make a portion of our mailing list available to reputable third parties that offer products we believe may interest you. If you prefer that we not exchange your name with third parties, or if you wish to clarify or modify your communication preferences, please visit us at www.ReaderService.com/consumerschoice or write to us at Harlequin Reader Service Preference Service, P.O. Box 9062, Buffalo, NY 14269. Include your complete name and address.

LI13R

SPECIAL EXCERPT FROM

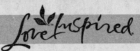

Don't miss a single book in the
BIG SKY CENTENNIAL *miniseries!*
Will rancher Jack McGuire and former love
Olivia Franklin find happily ever after in
HIS MONTANA SWEETHEART by Ruth Logan Herne?
Here's a sneak peek:

"We used to count the stars at night, Jack. Remember that?"

Oh, he remembered, all right. They'd look skyward and watch each star appear, summer, winter, spring and fall, each season offering its own array, a blend of favorites. Until they'd become distracted by other things. Sweet things.

A sigh welled from somewhere deep within him, a quiet blooming of what could have been. "I remember."

They stared upward, side by side, watching the sunset fade to streaks of lilac and gray. Town lights began to appear north of the bridge, winking on earlier now that it was August. "How long are you here?"

Olivia faltered. "I'm not sure."

He turned to face her, puzzled.

"I'm between lives right now."

He raised an eyebrow, waiting for her to continue. She did, after drawn-out seconds, but didn't look at him. She kept her gaze up and out, watching the tree shadows darken and dim.

"I was married."

He'd heard she'd gotten married several years ago, but the "was" surprised him. He dropped his gaze to her left hand. No ring. No tan line that said a ring had been there this summer. A flicker that might be hope stirred in his chest, but entertaining those notions would get him nothing but trouble, so he blamed the strange feeling on the half-finished sandwich he'd wolfed down on the drive in.

You've eaten fast plenty of times before this and been fine. Just fine.

The reminder made him take a half step forward, just close enough to inhale the scent of sweet vanilla on her hair, her skin.

He shouldn't. He knew that. He knew it even as his hand reached for her hand, the left one bearing no man's ring, and that touch, the press of his fingers on hers, made the tiny flicker inside brighten just a little.

The surroundings, the trees, the thin-lit night and the sound of rushing water made him feel as if anything was possible, and he hadn't felt that way in a very long time. But here, with her?

He did. And it felt good.

Find out what else is going on in Jasper Gulch in HIS MONTANA SWEETHEART by Ruth Logan Herne, available August 2014 from Love Inspired®.

Love Inspired

A reclusive Amish logger, Ethan Gingerich is more comfortable around his draft horses than the orphaned niece and nephews he's taken in. Yet he's determined to provide the children with a good, loving home. The little ones, including a defiant eight-year-old, need a proper nanny. But when Ethan hires shy Amishwoman Clara Barkman, he never expects her temporary position to have such a lasting hold on all of them. Now this man of few words must convince Clara she's found her forever home and family.

BRIDES OF
Amish Country

Finding true love in the land of the Plain People.

The Amish Nanny

by

Patricia Davids

Available August 2014 wherever
Love Inspired books and ebooks are sold.

LI87902